The Augur

SEEING DEATH

L.M. SOMERTON

ENTWINED PUBLISHING

Seeing Death
ISBN # 978-1-80250-259-6
©Copyright L.M. Somerton 2025
Cover Art by Kelly Martin ©Copyright September 2025
Interior text design by Entwined Publishing
Published by Eternal, an Entwined Publishing imprint

Published in 2025 by Entwined Publishing, United Kingdom.

Entwined Publishing is a division of Totally Entwined Group Limited.

SEEING DEATH

Dedication

To being a little different.

Prologue

"Your parents would have been very proud of the young man you've become, Bryn. You're going to love college."

Bryn Ashton cupped his mug of hot chocolate and eyed his housemother warily. "I sense a but coming on."

"Buuuut…can you please curb that sharp tongue of yours. Make some friends. Be nice."

"I knew the marshmallows on the top of this were a bribe."

"Bryn…"

"I know! I only get one chance and I won't mess up, promise. That's if I don't turn into some monster freak tomorrow. There used to be a time when people looked forward to their eighteenth birthdays, right?"

Annie Cormac shook her head. "In the thirty years I've been running group homes, I've not had a single kid turn into a monster. A couple of werewolves and one vamp. That's it. All three of them have gone on to successful careers and happy lives. They are *not* monsters. No one affected by the gene mutation is, and I won't have you using that word in this house."

"Sorry, Annie."

"I should think so. I know the virus killing your parents has been hard but remember, they were part of the team that found the cure."

"I don't remember them, you know that. I was a baby when they died, and no different from thousands of other kids whose parents were taken. I'm not complaining."

"Fifty years to find a cure. So many deaths."

"And so many people with traits we all thought were the stuff of movies and books. What if I…"

"None of that now. Even if you do turn out to be lupine or sanguine, it'll make little difference. You'll have to take an additional minor at college is all, so that you learn to cope with the changes to your body. A good portion of men in the military, police force and fire service are wolves now. Vamps make great doctors and scientists."

"But what if I'm…different?"

"Oh, honey, other changes are so rare that's very unlikely. You'll wake up tomorrow and be your usual grumpy self."

"I can't imagine how much of a crap fest it would be to discover you can suddenly read minds or predict the future like some kind of oracle."

"Which is why people like that have to be protected by the authorities. How many seers or augurs have you heard of in your lifetime? I can only recall one, so stop worrying. You've got more chance of winning the lottery."

"I guess. How does the gene even know when a person reaches eighteen? Is it in there putting crosses on a calendar or something—like its counting down to Christmas?"

"That's one of several mysteries yet to be solved. Same as why the virus was only fatal to certain age groups while others didn't even know they had it, and why the virus only activates the gene in males."

"There'll be lots of kids like me at college, won't there?"

"Sure will. Fifty percent of kids in your generation grew up in group homes just like this one."

Bryn drained his mug. "I want tomorrow to be over so I can get back to worrying about my college roommate turning out to be a trombone player. Normal stuff." He shoved his chair back. "Thanks for the chocolate, Annie. I'll be in my room embracing my Goth tendencies."

"Keep the volume down." Annie pulled him into a hug. "What will be, will be, Bryn. Try to get some sleep."

Bryn left the familiar warmth of the kitchen and climbed the three flights of stairs to his attic room. As the current oldest ward of the group home, he had a room to himself. Everyone else had to share, which he'd also had to do until the previous eldest had moved out two years before. In a house full of noisy kids ranging in age from four to seventeen, his room was his sanctuary. It was a quiet place to study and to dream. He couldn't wait to leave for college and the government funded full-ride scholarship that would allow him to study biochemistry. One day he wanted to join the team researching the effects of the virus that had taken his parents. The cure was a recent discovery and, though future generations might be protected by infant vaccination, it didn't work on those who had already turned.

It was getting late and he should sleep. Tomorrow there would be a cake and gifts, even though for him the celebration would be tinged with sadness. Reaching eighteen meant that his time at the group home was coming to an end. It was all he'd ever known, but he had his college place and in two weeks would be moving on. He had to pack up his life into a few boxes and leave Annie and the other kids behind. It was exciting and terrifying at the same time.

His room was a reflection of his personality. The walls were covered with posters of indie rock bands begged from the downtown record store. His shelves were stacked with an eclectic mix of books on topics as diverse as archeology to zoology and fiction covering everything from horror and thrillers to the classics. Reading had always been an escape and Bryn's part-time job bagging groceries at the neighborhood store had funded his addiction.

He picked up a framed photo of his parents. The smiling people staring back at him were strangers, but he had inherited his mother's black hair and his father's green eyes and pale skin. The mixture of Irish and Hispanic heritage from generations back had come through strong in him. He'd been a late child, a welcome surprise after years of trying, and because of that his grandparents had all passed on. Neither of his parents had any siblings, which meant that when the virus took them, he was left alone. If he had any relatives anywhere, he didn't know about them and presumably they had no idea he existed. No one had ever tried to claim him.

After kicking off his battered boots, Bryn stretched out on his bed. He didn't undress because he had yet to make a pre-sleep trip to the bathroom, which was on the floor below. He had on black jeans and a black T-shirt—there were no other colors in his wardrobe. He spotted a hole in one sock and wiggled a pale toe. *Maybe vamping out wouldn't be too bad.* He tongued an incisor. *It's not like sanguines turn into bats or anything, just need more red meat than most and high factor sunscreen. Don't think I'd make a great wolf though, they're way too energetic.* Those with the wolf gene were stronger, faster and usually hairier than an average human. They did not howl at the moon, silver didn't kill them and they didn't turn into slavering beasts. No painful bone cracking or shredding of clothes. *All the myths and legends are a crock of shit but they have to mean that the genes have been active in the past. They must have been dormant and the virus reactivated them somehow.* That was the working theory anyhow. Meanwhile, boys reaching maturity continued to approach their birthdays with trepidation.

"Annie's right, of course. Fuck all I can do about it," Bryn grumbled. He cracked a yawn and took that as a signal to head for the bathroom. Morning would come soon enough and he wanted to face it with a clear head.

* * * *

"Nightmares suck." A few short hours later, Bryn lay in bed staring at the ceiling. A crack in the plaster traveled the full width of the room. Bryn had named it San Andreas and had watched its progress over the last two years with morbid curiosity, wondering if he'd wake one morning covered in plaster and looking at the sky. Light filtered through the institutional gray blinds, telling him his birthday had arrived. *Hmm, don't feel any different.* He raised one arm. Not any hairier. A peek beneath the covers showed him a chest still bereft of a single, solitary hair. "Not a wolf then." He prodded his teeth. They didn't seem any pointier than usual and he wasn't craving raw steak for breakfast. "Not a vamp either. Wow. Totally normal. Whatever that is." Pushing away the remnants of his bad dream from his mind, he swung his legs out of bed. He sat for a moment, shrugged, then went through his usual morning routine before dressing and heading for the kitchen.

The moment he walked in, ten eager faces turned his way. Expressions ranged from boredom to curiosity to outright fascination. Bryn held up a hand. "Before any of you brats say a word, no, not a wolf, not a vamp. Just me."

He was swarmed by a crowd of kids who all apparently needed to check him over in person. Summoning his last ounce of patience, he stood still for an entire minute before shedding them. The youngest he tucked under one arm before depositing her on a chair where she dissolved in giggles.

"Annie, please tell me there's coffee."

"Do I look like your maid? It's in the pot. Pancakes are on the way."

Bryn dragged himself to the coffee pot, poured a mug, downed it then got himself a refill before he resumed his seat. He was no longer the center of attention and conversations carried on around him. He poured juice for the little ones then broke up a fight over the cereal boxes. His head pounded.

"Didn't sleep well, huh?" Annie deposited a plate of fluffy pancakes in front of him. "Birthday boy gets the first stack."

"Thanks, Annie, and no, I didn't. Weird dreams."

The familiar chaos of breakfast carried on around Bryn and he let it wash over him. The other kids were great but his tolerance was limited, particularly first thing in the morning. Annie slid two Tylenol his way.

"Lifesaver." He swallowed the tablets with more coffee.

"You should switch to decaf and I can't believe I need to say that to an eighteen year old." Annie waved a batter-coated spatula at him.

"Noted."

Next came gifts. There were pictures and crafts from the littlies and the three biggest had pooled a few dollars to get him a black ceramic takeout cup with a skull and cross bones on it. "I love it." Bryn was genuinely touched. "It'll be so useful at school. Thanks, guys."

Annie gave him a hand-knitted black scarf with a single pale blue line across each end. "It'll get cold at Harvard." She hugged him and suddenly he was mobbed with lots of warm bodies, all demanding hugs. Tears pricked at his eyes.

"You guys! Stop!" The kids drifted away and Bryn was left with Annie. "That was...sweet."

"They like you, despite that emo façade you put on."

"Hey!"

"We'll have cake after dinner tonight, okay?"

"Yeah. I'm full of pancakes now."

"I've put a little money in the bank account we set up for you...no arguing, it's what you're due. A little kick-starter for college books, that kind of thing."

"I don't know what to say. Thank you."

"That'll do. How's the head?"

"Pounding. Strange—I don't tend to get headaches." Bryn knuckled his temples. "Think I'll go lie down. Try to catch up on some of the sleep I didn't get last night. Now I know I'm not...special."

"You'll always be special to me, sweet cheeks." Annie ruffled his hair.

Bryn made gagging noises. "Stop already!"

"Go to bed."

The next thing Bryn knew was someone shaking him awake. He groaned and cranked an eyelid. "Annie?"

"Hey, Sleeping Beauty. You've been out cold for eight hours. You need to get your rear downstairs." Annie yanked open the drapes, flooding the room with light. "I hope you haven't picked up the flu or something."

"Ow, fuck!" Bryn hid beneath the covers. Sleep had not improved his headache.

"Language, young man. The screening bureau officer is downstairs eating my cookies. You need to come show him the gene hasn't activated."

"Sorry. Okay. On it. Give me two seconds." He winced at the door closing, the noise pounding his skull like a jackhammer. He grabbed his shades and put them on. Gently. Shielding his eyes from the light helped a bit. *Must have been more stressed out about today than I realized. This has to be a migraine.*

Bryn counted it a win that he made it down the stairs without falling on his ass. Annie was waiting with the official in the TV room. They were both seated on the sectional, chattering away like old pals.

"Here he is, Charlie. The latest of a long line."

"And no indications?"

"None. He's his normal teenage self."

"Oh dear. Congratulations on your birthday, Bryn. I'm Charles Donovan from the screening bureau and this visit is nothing to worry about." He held out a hand and Bryn shook it.

"Hey."

"I'm going to give you a finger prick for a blood sample. It's a quick and easy test for gene activation which shows us sanguine or lupine indications. A visual assessment isn't always accurate."

Bryn slumped on the sectional, trying not to look as belligerent as he felt. "This is pointless."

"Probably," Charlie said. "But wouldn't you rather have it noted on your record that you have no active gene so that you don't have people hounding you in the future?"

"I suppose."

"Be nice, Bryn." Annie's warning tone was enough to have him sitting a bit straighter.

Charlie got out his testing kit. "Don't worry, you won't miss the tiny bit I'm going to take." He jabbed Bryn's middle finger pad then collected a bead of blood on a dropper that went into a tiny test tube of clear liquid. "It's red at least."

"You say that to everyone, don't you?" Bryn muttered.

"Sure do. Perk of the job. Right, I'm looking for what color the liquid changes to. Lupine goes green, sanguine is purple. No gene change is golden yellow." He shook the tube.

"So what the fuck is sky blue?" Bryn felt sick. He stared at the little glass vial.

"I...need to make a call. Don't move." Charlie went into the hall.

Bryn watched him go. "Annie, what's happening?"

"I don't know." She came to sit next to him on the couch and grabbed his hand.

A pulse of sharp pain shot through Bryn's already throbbing head and his vision dimmed. In his head he had a picture of Annie standing in the dock of a courtroom facing a judge. She looked resigned. Bryn yanked his hand away in horror and the image faded.

"If you go now, you'll have time to grab a few things and get out through the back yard," Annie whispered. "I'll tell Charlie you went to the bathroom."

"What? Why would I do that?"

"Because if that test is showing that you have some rare variation of the gene, you'll be taken by the security services and put through God knows what kind of experimentation while they work out what you can do."

"And if I run, they'll hunt me down. When you touched me Annie, I saw...well, let's just say things wouldn't work out well for you either." It was tempting to try it. Bryn thought he could make a good go of disappearing, but he couldn't do that to Annie. If she was blamed, what would happen to all the other kids in her care? He wasn't that much of an asshole.

"You shouldn't think about me. I'd happily go to court for you. Be selfish. Go."

Bryn slumped on the couch. "No. Not an option." Tentatively, he touched Annie's hand. He flinched at the pain but now the image in his head was of a smiling Annie watching over kids playing in the yard. His vision cleared and he sighed. "I guess Harvard is off the cards. Fuck."

When Charlie came back into the room, he seemed tense. "Your test result is...unusual, Bryn. You felt fine this morning?"

"Yeah, apart from a headache. I didn't sleep well last night. It got worse, though."

"Do you know what time you were born?"

"Eight-thirty in the morning," Annie contributed. "It's in his records."

"Gene activation can be very precise. The change must have happened after you got up this morning. Would you take off your sunglasses for me?"

Hand trembling, Bryn removed the glasses. The light hurt his eyes.

"Oh my." Annie stared at him.

"What?" Panicked, Bryn went to look in the mirror on the mantel over the fire. "Fuck me." His eyes were a far brighter shade of green than they had been and they seemed backlit, glowing like a cat's in the dark. He put the glasses back on. "They weren't like that earlier."

"There'll be a car here for you shortly. More tests will need to be done. I can come with you to your room, if you want to pack a few things."

"When will I be back?" Bryn asked the question even though he already knew the answer.

"Not sure. It could be a while."

He means never. Why me? Bryn wanted to scream but decided it would hurt his head too much. "Fine. You and the kids will have to share that cake, Annie."

Charlie trailed him up the stairs then stood in the doorway while Bryn threw a few things in a duffel.

"You thought about running, didn't you?"

"Maybe."

"What stopped you?"

"Annie's been the closest thing to a mother I've ever had. She doesn't deserve trouble because of me."

"Yeah, she's one of the good ones."

"Has this ever happened to you before… I mean the blue reaction?"

"Never. I've had a few wolves in my time and one or two vamps. This was new."

"Great. Just fucking great." *Should have bought that lottery ticket.*

"You done? Let's go see if the car's here."

Some of the other kids had gathered in the hall. There was a clamor of questions. Annie ushered them away and raised a hand in farewell. "Good luck," she mouthed.

Bryn gave her what he hoped was a reassuring smile rather than a grimace. When the door closed behind him, it had an air of finality.

"They're here," Charlie announced.

A black SUV with heavily tinted windows drew up at the curb. Two armed men in black fatigues got out and one walked over. The other stayed by the vehicle, scanning the street as if he expected an attack to come out of nowhere at any moment.

"This him?" the man addressed Charlie.

"What am I, invisible?" Bryn muttered.

"It is. I sent through his test result already." Charlie took a step back.

"He give you any trouble?"

"Seriously? Does it look like I did?" Bryn made a conscious effort not to be intimidated by the excessive amount of firearms the guy carried.

"Get in the fucking car."

"A please wouldn't go amiss." Bryn stomped down the path. He tossed his duffel into the back seat then climbed in after it. He was followed by one of the men in black and before Bryn could come up with a suitable epithet, the guy stuck him with a needle. "What the actual…" He didn't get to finish the sentence before the lights went out.

* * * *

Bryn came around with a start. He wasn't sure what had woken him but had a vague sense that it had been a sharp noise. His headache had faded a bit but he was groggy and confused. "Where the fuck am I?" He was sitting on a plastic chair, head lolling, in a room that was in serious need of interior decoration. The gray walls were less than inviting. There was one door and a large interior window across one wall. He lifted his head, wincing at the crack his neck gave. *Has to be an interrogation room. There are probably people behind that window watching me.* It was then he realized that his wrists were cable-tied together. *This just gets better and better.* He raised both hands then gave the window the finger. *Juvenile, I know, but it makes me feel better.* There was a table in front of him so he laid his head on his arms and closed his eyes. *They'd better not have lost my shades.*

A few minutes later, the door opened. Footsteps crossed the room and someone occupied the chair on the other side of the table. Bryn's curiosity got the better of him and he raised his head. The man facing him looked to be in his forties, with silver-flecked dark hair and gray eyes. Everything about him was nondescript, as if he dressed deliberately to blend into the background. He pinned Bryn with a sharp gaze.

"How are you feeling, Bryn?"

"Like someone drugged me without my permission," Bryn muttered. "Where am I?"

"You were drugged specifically so that you wouldn't know your location. It means you can't tell anyone else and that helps us protect you."

"Protect me from what, exactly?"

"If you turn out to be what we think you are, it makes you valuable. Criminal elements will want to get their hands on you and at the moment, you're defenseless."

"So why are my hands tied? Unless you guys have a bondage fetish?"

"That's to stop you accidentally touching someone. It makes you more aware of where your hands are."

"And you don't want me touching anyone because…"

"We think you may be an augur."

Bryn stared at him. "And what exactly is that?"

"I think you already know that. There have been two examples in the last thirty years of blue tests like the one you had today. Both of those people were able to see the future in some way. One could also look into past memories." The man paused. "Charlie told me that he thought you'd already experienced something like that today. Tell me about that."

"How about you tell me who you are and why I should trust you, because I have to say, you're not making the best first impression."

"I work for the government, Bryn. For the organization that monitors and takes care of those who are gene gifted."

"Gifted. Right. You have a name?"

"Call me Warden or Sir, whichever you prefer."

"I wish I hadn't asked."

"The more cooperative you are, Bryn, the easier things will be. Now tell me what happened this morning."

Bryn sighed. He didn't want to spend more time than was necessary on the uncomfortable chair. "My housemother, Annie…after we saw the test this morning, she grabbed my hand. In my mind, I saw her in a courtroom. Then, after I realized that trying to get away is what would put her there, and I decided not to run, I touched her again. The images changed and she was safe and happy."

The warden grunted. "Sounds like you saw her future intent. And you haven't had visions about anyone else since?"

Bryn shook his head. "Nope, but your thugs knocked me out, remember?"

"Okay, this is what's going to happen. You'll be taken from here to a training facility. A kind of school, if you like. There, specialists will endeavor to gauge your abilities and test them. Alongside that you will receive a college-level education, a health and fitness program and psychological support."

"And I guess I get no choice in the matter?"

"None. This is a government requirement for somebody like you, and is all clearly defined in law."

"And how long am I supposed to stay at this place?"

"Between two and three years, depending on your progress and the strength of your abilities."

"And after that?"

"To be determined. Potentially, a job in the security services."

"What do the other people who tested blue do now?"

"They don't. They didn't survive their training."

On that note, Warden stood and left the room. Bryn stared at the closed door. *Wonderful. I am well and truly fucked.*

Chapter One

Three years later
Boston, Mass.

Detective Gunnar Ericson sat in the passenger seat of his unmarked pool Chevy and checked his watch. "It's almost midnight, they'd better be paying us overtime for this shit show."

"You gonna turn into a pumpkin when the clock strikes twelve?" Gunnar's partner, Detective Maeve O'Riordan, grabbed another donut from the box on the dash and adjusted her position behind the wheel.

"Did you take the last jelly one?" Gunnar prodded the remaining selection.

"Yep. Pregnancy privileges." Maeve patted her rounded belly. "Gotta take advantage while I can."

"You've been taking advantage since you knew you'd conceived. Does Cash know what a monster he's created?"

"He went out last night to buy me pickled eggs. At two a.m."

"True love."

"Shit. That's him, isn't it?" Maeve threw the donut box on the rear seat. "Guy on the left."

Gunnar stared at the two men exiting the casino he and Maeve had been staking out. As a lupine, or wolf, he had far superior eyesight to someone without the active gene, especially in low light conditions and at night. He had a wide field of view, excellent peripheral vision, and could detect the slightest motion. "Good spot. I'll go get him. You take the car to the end of the block. If he runs, he won't get any further than that."

"Deal. No biting."

"Funny." Gunnar levered his six-feet-five-inch frame out of the vehicle. He made it half way across the street before he was spotted and the suspect took off. Gunnar grinned. "I do love it when they run." He loped away in pursuit and hadn't reached anywhere close to his top speed before he caught the guy, bringing him down with a full-length tackle around the knees. "Guess what, asshole? You're under arrest."

Maeve pulled up alongside him and leaned out of the car window. "Can I be of assistance?"

"I'll let you arrest this idiot, as it's your last day and all," Gunnar said as he got to his feet, dragging the perp with him. He cuffed him before shoving him against the car.

"Coolio. I called in a black and white to come pick him up." Maeve read the guy his rights in a bored tone. "Out of interest, why did ya run? Have you been taking your own meth? You had to know he'd bring you down in seconds. I mean…look at him."

"Goddam wolves." The guy spat on the sidewalk.

"Ooh, you want me to add hate speech to your rap sheet?"

"Fuck you, lady."

"I'll take that as a yes. My work here is done." She polished her nails on her sleeve.

They waited until a couple of uniformed cops showed up to take charge of their prisoner then headed for the precinct.

"I am so ready for this shift to be over," Maeve said, pulling into an empty spot in the parking lot.

"Me too. Boss said he wants to speak to me in the morning, which is never good. Guess I'll get a new partner for a while." Gunnar leaned across to give Maeve a hug. "You get off, I'll finish up the paperwork."

"And that's why I love ya. Also, I hid a piece of my goodbye cake in the back of the breakroom fridge for you."

"Chances of that still being there…"

"It's in a box marked fecal samples."

"Your future kid has a genius for a mom."

"He/she/they sure does."

Gunnar gave her a final kiss then made his way inside. At one in the morning, the homicide squad room was quiet. Two guys on the night shift gave him weary waves then carried on doing whatever it was they were pretending to work on. Gunnar headed for the breakroom and retrieved his cake, holding his breath to avoid his sensitive nose getting a whiff of out-of-date yogurt and a stale salami sandwich. He rejected the suspect liquid in the coffeepot for a glass of water then returned to his desk. He was done with both his cake and his report by one-thirty and was about to leave when one of his colleagues ambled over.

"Hey, Gunnar, I hear they have someone new lined up for you tomorrow."

"I guess so. Maeve is off to do baby stuff. What did you hear? Tell me I'm not getting someone straight out of the Academy."

"All I heard was fresh and green. Other than that, the grapevine is silent."

"That sounds like spinach or maybe broccoli, neither of which I'm fond of. I'll guess I'll find out in the morning, which is too close for comfort. These late-night stakeouts are a killer. I need to get home and crash, grab a few hours shuteye at least."

"Maybe you'll get a vamp."

"Not many vamp cops around here. They're cool anyway."

"Until they start sucking on your jugular."

"Cut it out with that bullshit, Evans. Next thing you'll be trying to convince us all the earth is flat." Gunnar gave a low warning growl.

Evans backed away. "Yeah, yeah, I didn't mean anything by it. It's late and I'm tired."

Gunnar gave him a brief nod. "Hope your shift is uneventful." It was too late to start something with Evans, who had a reputation for being denser than the average cinder block. Gunnar headed for the parking lot where his Harley was stowed in a narrow space next to a dumpster where there was no chance it would get dinged by some asshole rookie who couldn't drive. The pool Chevy was great for stakeouts but Gunnar far preferred his bike.

He zipped up his leather jacket then threw a leg across the saddle. He got comfortable before firing up the ignition. The low rumble of the powerful engine always made him smile. He put his helmet on, because even wolves didn't win in a fight with the asphalt. He tucked his long hair into his collar to stop it flying around then headed into the city to home and much needed rest.

* * * *

He was back the next morning after four hours' sleep, in a mood that could best be described as belligerent. There wasn't enough coffee in the world to deal with his sleep deprivation, but he gave it a shot. A triple shot of espresso in fact. He bought it from the coffee wagon that had a pitch on the other side of the fence from the parking lot. The guy that ran it, Asa, understood his customer base. He provided caffeine, sugar, decent burgers and large portion sizes to needy cops at reasonable prices. He didn't engage in unnecessary conversation, which suited Gunnar.

He was inhaling his coffee when he walked into the squad room. He didn't make it to his desk before his captain beckoned him into his glass-walled office, which took up one corner of the floor.

"That was a good collar last night. Nice work." Captain Jacobson, mid-fifties and bald as a cue ball, sank into his chair.

Gunnar eyed him suspiciously. "The last time you complimented me on an arrest, you'd sent me to a crime scene where the victim was in twelve separate pieces. You ruined my appetite. So spill, what's going on?"

"You're being seconded."

"What the actual fuck? Maeve's been gone all of five minutes."

"Keep your hair on and let me finish. My understanding is that you'll still be working homicide, just with a different, specialist unit that's going to be attached to us for a while. It's a trial thing."

"What specialist unit?"

"Need to know, and apparently I don't yet. I've got an address and you need to get your ass over there by nine. You'll be briefed when you arrive. Try to act like you were socialized as a kid, okay?"

"This sucks. What about giving me a say?"

"It comes with a special duty allowance. Another two grand a month."

"Can we stick with the whole how about asking me thing?"

Captain Jacobson glared at him. "You think I had any choice? I don't know who the fuck picked you, but they did, God help them. Be your usual insubordinate self and they'll probably kick your butt back over here within the week."

Gunnar grunted. "Give me the fucking address."

"Here." The captain handed him a piece of paper torn out of a notepad. "Memorize it. Shred it."

Gunnar gave him a final scowl before stomping back to his desk, muttering under his breath. He was sorely tempted to be late but one look at the mountain of paperwork on his desk changed his mind. He checked the address, put the piece of paper in the shredder then retraced his steps to the parking lot.

Marlborough Street was in the heart of the upscale Back Bay area and when Gunnar reached the address he found himself outside a well-kept but unremarkable townhouse. There was nothing outside to indicate that it was anything other than a residential property but as he approached the door, it swung open. The bespectacled woman standing on the step gave him a condescending look.

"You may put your machine around back. Left, left again. Look for the number on the gate in the alley." She shut the door in his face.

"Nice to meet you too." Gunnar took a slow ride around the block to the back yard, wheeled his bike inside then rested it on the kickstand. An older man with short silvering hair stood at the back door to the property.

"Detective Ericson, thank you for being prompt. I'm Warden."

"Mr. Warden... are you gonna tell me what I'm doing here?" *Look at me being polite.*

"It's just Warden, and yes, I am. Please come inside and I can introduce you to your new partner."

This is some seriously weird shit. Gunnar trailed the man along a thickly carpeted hallway then into an office. Its furnishings were surprisingly utilitarian considering the plush feel of the property. Metal filing cabinets ran along one wall and a desk sat in front of the barred window. In one corner was a low table encircled by three leather chairs. There were three glasses on the table, along with a bottle of water.

"Take a seat please, Detective. Help yourself to a drink. I'll be back shortly."

Gunnar poured himself a glass of water more for something to do than anything. He didn't do well with sitting still so wandered across to the filing cabinets. He tested a couple of drawers but they were locked. The only view out of the window was of a brick wall and the top of the desk was clear. There were no clues in the room to its occupant or the organization he worked for.

The sound of low voices reached his sharp ears a while before the office door opened. Warden was first to come inside, followed by a striking young man. He was dressed entirely in black, had black hair and pale skin. He also had on very dark sunglasses, which was peculiar considering it wasn't that bright in the room.

Gunnar stared at him with blatant curiosity. *Doesn't smell like a vamp, but there's something about him...*

"Detective Gunnar Ericson, I'd like you to meet Bryn Ashton, your new partner," Warden stated.

"Hi, I guess," Gunnar said, holding out his hand.

"Hi, yourself." It wasn't until Bryn shook his hand that Gunnar noticed he was wearing tightfitting leather gloves.

Warden looked at Bryn then at Gunnar. "Sit down, gentlemen."

Gunnar had to admit that his curiosity needed satisfying. He took a seat. Warden joined him then, after a moment's hesitation, so did Bryn.

He's young, can't be more than early twenties. But what the fuck is he?

"I can see you have questions, Detective, and they will be answered, but first I have to ask you to sign a statement agreeing to keep everything you learn here completely confidential. Will that be a problem?" Warden extracted an envelope from his inside jacket pocket. He took out a single sheet of paper and put it on the table in front of Gunnar along with a silver pen. Gunnar took his time reading it, but it was fairly standard. He'd seen similar before working cases that involved other government agencies. He signed at the bottom then pushed the piece of paper back to Warden.

"Not a problem."

"Thank you. Very well, I would imagine that your wolf senses have detected that Bryn is neither wolf nor vampire. That's because he is an augur."

"Fucking hell." Gunnar had not seen that coming.

"Quite." Warden was too polite to roll his eyes, but Gunnar sensed he wanted to.

"Are you sure this was the best Boston PD had to offer?" Bryn's tone had a sharp edge. "Because I'm not seeing it so far."

"Be nice, Bryn. You're going to be working and living with the detective, so I suggest you curb your tone."

"Wait, what?" Gunnar thought he must've misheard. "What do you mean *living with*?"

"I understand that this is all something of a shock to you, Detective, but hear me out. As I said, Bryn is an augur. An extremely gifted one. He's rare and as such highly valuable. His...*abilities* match well with police work, and I'll explain more about that shortly, but the partner he works with also has to keep him safe. Once his existence becomes known in criminal circles, he'll be in constant danger."

"So why not keep him hidden? Keep him safe?"

"Because the law does not allow us to keep him prisoner, Detective. Legislation gave us three years to train him, which we have done. We also have the right to secure his services for the government. But, we have to allow him a life. Living together isn't compulsory but it would be easier for you. Bryn has been given a secure apartment at the top of this building, which will also be at your disposal. You will escort him at all times when you are at work. He is never, and I can't emphasize this enough, never to be left alone outside of this building or a secure premises. Do you understand?"

"I get it, but I didn't sign up for this. I was told I was joining a specialist unit attached to Boston PD."

"Yes...we had to have a reasonable story to give your superiors. You'll be working with a range of law enforcement agencies including Boston PD."

"Why me?"

"The question I ask myself every goddamned day," Bryn muttered. "Welcome to the asylum."

"You've brought down some very nasty people, Detective. You also have close protection experience. We needed someone with a reputation for being trustworthy and it had to be a wolf. Your enhanced senses and physical advantages will make Bryn safer."

"And if I graciously decline this opportunity?"

"You'll go back to your precinct and Bryn will return to the secure training facility whilst we identify another partner for him. How about I leave you two alone for a while? You can get to know each other."

"Sure." Gunnar was curious if nothing else.

Bryn shrugged. "Whatever."

Warden left the room, closing the door behind him. "He looked anxious," Gunnar commented.

"He thinks I'll piss you off and you'll walk," Bryn said.

"I wonder what gives him that idea." Gunnar's tone oozed sarcasm. "What's with the shades?"

In response, Bryn took them off. His green eyes glowed, cat-like. "Another neat side-effect of being a freak."

"Wow." Gunnar leaned closer. Bryn smelled of fresh apples. "Does everything look green to you?"

"Nope. Normal vision."

"And do they do that all the time?"

"Pretty much." Bryn gripped the arm of his seat, leather tight across his knuckles.

"Okay. You get to ask me a question now."

"So you're a wolf?"

"Yep. Why are you wearing gloves?"

"Wait, I didn't get to ask…"

"You asked a question. I answered. My turn."

"My abilities work through touch. Has to be skin-to-skin contact. I have to be careful."

"Fair enough."

"What does being a wolf mean?"

"I'm strong, fast, my senses are sharper than normal. I like chasing stuff, it's the wolf desire to hunt prey coming through."

"So if I threw a ball…"

"That's another question, but no, you little brat, I won't be running after your ball, Frisbee or any other random projectile." Gunnar played with a loose thread on the hem of his T-shirt. "So what can you do?"

"I can tell if someone is lying. I can see possible futures for a person that reflect their intent and their past, if violence or very strong emotion was involved. The memory has to have power."

"I can see why you have value to law enforcement. Interrogating scumbags would be a whole lot easier with you around."

"Do you have family?" Bryn asked.

"No. Group home kid. Parents didn't survive the virus and I was their only child." Gunnar released his hair from its tie, shaking it out around his shoulders. "You?"

"Same. It was okay, though. I had a great housemother."

"Do you want to touch me?" Gunnar asked, grinning.

"That's a fucking leading question."

"You're too young for me…if you're even into men, and that's not what I meant and you know it. You're not too young to put over my knee."

"That's…you're…fuck." Bryn stripped off his gloves. "Give me your arm. Pulse point in the wrist works better than the hand, too many bones."

Gunnar complied and Bryn gripped his wrist. His fingers were surprisingly cool. Gunnar watched his face intently. "You're truthful. You're...wow, you're going to take the gig and oh..." Bryn let go, his forehead creased. He put his glasses back on.

"That hurt you."

"Yeah. I'm used to it."

"You should have said. I wouldn't have suggested it if I'd known. You saw something else, what was it?"

"I'm not telling you that." There was a stubborn set to Bryn's lips.

His pink, plump lips. Gunnar had a good idea what Bryn had seen. The telltale bulge in his pants was a giveaway. *Interesting. Wonder if it was spanking or sex.* "Well, I'm in. You need someone who isn't going to take any of your angsty crap and you can keep your gloves off around me. I'm an open book. No secrets. The eyes don't bother me either."

Bryn's shoulders dropped and he sat back in his seat. He'd clenched his hands in his lap and now his fingers relaxed.

"Didn't want to go back to the Facility, huh?"

"No."

There was a world of meaning in that single snapped word. "Have you moved into the apartment yet?"

"Most of my stuff is here but I didn't want to go see it in case things didn't work out with you."

Protecting himself. He's tougher than he looks. "So you wanna go take a look around?"

"I guess."

Gunnar had no idea where to go so he gestured for Bryn to lead the way. They passed Warden in the corridor. He gave Gunnar a speculative glance but didn't comment.

The townhouse was four stories and the entire top floor had been converted into a self-contained apartment. Bryn poked his head into every room, more animated than Gunnar had seen him so far. There was a small but well-equipped kitchen with a table on one side, two bedrooms — each with an attached bathroom — an L-shaped sitting room with a dining table and chairs in the smaller section and a study set up with two desks, computers and shelves already stacked with books.

"I got to pick out bedding, flatware and stuff," Bryn said. "I only had a single room at the Facility."

"It's comfortable. You can add more homey touches over time. Who owns this building?"

"It's the headquarters of an organization called GCR, Gene Control & Research. Warden is the boss. Its government funded and is responsible for monitoring all gene research into wolves and vamps. They set legislation around gene-active people and decide what happens to people like me."

"What color did you test?"

"Blue."

"Didn't know that was a thing," Gunnar admitted. "I know wolves and vamps test in different shades of the same colors depending on the strength of their gene traits."

"There was a constant flow of both through the Facility. Not resident, though."

Gunnar wandered into one of the bedrooms and tested the bounce of the mattress. "So, do you want this place to yourself? I'm easy either way. I won't be offended if you want some space. I need to find out where we'll be working from, but I can come pick you up."

Bryn pushed his shades onto his head. "It'll be easier if you're here because this will be our base. Warden will put a guard outside if he thinks I'll try to go out on my own."

"What's to stop you making a run for it?" Gunnar asked. "They can't watch you every second, you're not a prisoner."

"This place and the job are conditional on me 'not putting myself at risk'," Bryn said. "They also surgically implanted a tracking device into my spine. In case they ever need to come rescue me from anyone that isn't them."

"That sucks."

"Yeah. My life is a bed of fucking roses."

"And now you get to work with me." Gunnar grinned.

"Just fucking peachy."

Bryn wanted to stay in the apartment and do some unpacking, so Gunnar left him to it and went to find Warden. He suspected Bryn needed to be alone for a while. *I can't even begin to imagine what's he's been through the last few years. It's a miracle he's still sane.*

Warden was in his study. The door was open so Gunnar went inside. Warden looked up from his work.

"So, Detective, have you decided to join us?"

"The kid intrigues me. It'll be interesting to see how he can help with solving cases, so yeah, I'm in. I'll need to make arrangements to get my stuff shipped over here."

"That will all be arranged for you," Warden said. "I need the key to your apartment and a list of items you want brought here. What will you do with the apartment?"

"Sublet, I guess," Gunnar said. "The place is rent controlled so I don't want to lose it in case things don't work out here."

"Fair enough. I can arrange a suitable tenant, if that's amenable?"

"That would help me out."

"We want your focus to be on the work rather than domestic affairs. This is experimental and dangerous. Initially we will offer your services across the city and you'll focus on interrogations for only the most serious offenses. If things go well, we'll consider expanding your remit to investigation, but we have to see how Bryn copes first. He's had a lot of practice honing his skills but not in real situations. Using his gifts can be draining and he's not so good at taking care of himself."

"Noted. So where's our first gig?"

"You'll be briefed tomorrow morning. The investigating team will come here to our conference room and once you've heard what they need, it will be up to you and Bryn to decide whether you want to take on the case. I'll arrange for a car to be at your disposal…"

"I'll use my bike. It's quicker in traffic and if I ever need to get Bryn out of a situation quickly, it'll work better. Can you get him a helmet and leathers?"

Warden gave a brief nod. "Certainly. There will be a car available as well, in case of need." He placed a sleek cell on the desk. "This is for you. There are several secure apps on there, including one linked to Bryn's tracker. We'll be asking you to report on each job, not just about the case but what you observe when Bryn works."

"Does he know about that? I won't spy on him for you," Gunnar said. "Partners need trust."

"He knows. You'll need to write the reports together so that he can relay any physical impact. Psychologically, we have no way of knowing how he'll be affected in the long term, but he'll have regular sessions with a counselor who's familiar with him already. His mental health is important. He's the first augur to survive training and by far the strongest. The others couldn't handle the strain of what they could do. One had a stroke, the other took his own life."

Gunnar was beginning to suspect that *his* life was about to get complicated. "His attitude is a defense mechanism. If he was a sensitive flower, he wouldn't make it."

"Quite. That doesn't mean you shouldn't call him out on bad behavior. You have seniority. He obeys your orders or there will be consequences." Warden steepled his fingers. "He's very young. He's developed an armored shell, but it's brittle. He needs careful but firm handling."

An image of what 'firm handling' might entail flashed through Gunnar's mind and his cock twitched. *He's too young, you fucking pervert. Get your head out of your pants and concentrate.* The devil on his shoulder was telling him that the age gap was only six years and that Bryn was exactly Gunnar's type. Feisty but vulnerable and so very pretty. *It's been too long since I got laid.* He tuned back in to Warden's ongoing lecture. Hopefully anything he'd missed would be written down in a manual somewhere.

"If you turn right out of here and go to the third office on the left, one of my staff will explain the security arrangements for this building, give you your new credentials, get some paperwork filled out, that kind of thing. Welcome to the team, Detective. I'm sure we've chosen the right man." He stood and offered his hand. Gunnar shook it, recognizing the dismissal.

"I'll do my best," he said, and meant it. It wasn't in him to do anything less. The future was going to be interesting. *And ain't that the understatement of the year.*

Chapter Two

That first night, Gunnar went back to his own place to check on the movers. He wasn't especially attached to his apartment but it had been home for four years. By the time he got there, the team was almost done. They'd packed his clothes and all the obviously personal items. He added a few throws and pillows he thought Bryn might like and made sure his French press went into a crate. Most stuff was staying for the new tenant as the Marlborough Street apartment was fully equipped. Gunnar had never been a pack rat. Accumulating stuff didn't interest him so his belongings were loaded and driven away in less than three hours. To avoid putting linens on the stripped beds, he camped out on the couch in a sleeping bag. He slept well and woke early, more excited than he had expected to be to begin his new job.

The back gate at Marlborough Street was locked this time and Gunnar had to use a code to get in. Another keypad got him through the rear entrance, a camera tracking his movements as he entered. Warden emerged from his office as Gunnar passed.

"I'll walk with you to the conference room. Your belongings were safely delivered last night and have been taken up to the apartment. You'll be staying here from tonight?"

"That bridge is burned. If I want clean underwear tomorrow, I need in those boxes."

"Quite. At least you'll have a short commute."

"Does anyone else live on site here?"

"Other than you and Bryn, not permanently, but we have some rooms for staff to use as needed. As there's a study in your apartment, I've not set up another office for you down here. Your computer has access to everything you'll need. If the space isn't adequate, let me know."

"Sure. So what do we have this morning?"

"We're keeping it close for your first case. It's the local FBI office rather than Boston PD. Nasty serial killer case. You've heard of the Forest Ripper?"

"The press sure do love to dream up dramatic names, don't they? Yeah, I've heard of him. Can't imagine there's a cop who hasn't. Psycho takes young boys off the street in Boston, dumps their bodies weeks later, always in forest areas around the city."

"That's the one. I'll let the team brief you. It'll be a rough start for Bryn but that's the job."

When Gunnar walked into the conference room his eyes were immediately drawn to Bryn, who was lounging in a chair at the far end of the table. Gunnar held back a grin. Bryn was definitely making some kind of statement with his outfit. He had on skintight ripped black jeans, biker boots and a faded band T-shirt. His sunglasses were in place but he wasn't wearing his gloves. Gunnar could see them tucked into the waistband of his jeans. The other occupants of the room were much more traditionally dressed in dark suits.

Warden assumed the seat at the head of the table and everyone followed his lead. Gunnar took the seat to one side of Bryn.

"Morning, partner."

Bryn scowled. "Well, aren't you the chirpy one this morning. I fell over a box of your crap before I'd had coffee."

"Should have looked where you were going then, shouldn't you?" Gunnar could sense Bryn's glare through his shades.

"There was also no sugar-coated cereal. Granola. They expect me to eat granola."

"Lodge a complaint with human resources."

"Fuck you."

"Shall we get started, gentlemen?" There was a warning in Warden's tone. Even the FBI agents sat up straighter. "Detective Ericson, Bryn, I'd like to introduce Special Agents Bell and Gomez. They will conduct this briefing."

One of the agents handed around slim manila folders. "This case spans several years so the information you have is a brief summary. There's also a picture of the man we believe to be the 'Forest Ripper', Dr. Everard Templeton. He's a long-term Boston resident and eminent surgeon at Boston General. His specialism is pediatric surgery."

Gunnar glanced up from the paperwork. "So why do you need us if you already have him?"

"The evidence is all circumstantial. He's a very clever man. Having an augur to call on is an absolute godsend. We don't want this guy back on the streets."

"Bryn is a certified level five augur, gentlemen. His evidence is admissible in all court proceedings. If this *is* your killer, he'll be able to confirm it." Warden pushed his chair back. "I'll leave you to carry on. Detective Ericson is in charge."

After Warden had left the room, Gunnar poured himself a glass of water. "I assume you *do* have Dr. Templeton in custody?"

Agent Bell nodded. "We only have another twelve hours before we either have to charge him or let him go. He's toying with us and enjoying it. You guys are a trump card I can't wait to play. Should wipe the sneer off his smug, superior face."

"No love lost then."

"He's been arrested twice before. His lawyer was a snake oil salesman in a previous life. Slippery as fuck."

"Bryn has to have skin-to-skin physical contact with your man. Is that likely to be risky?"

Agent Bell tapped his pen on the table. "No. He's icy calm, not hot tempered. I imagine he'll find an augur an intellectual curiosity."

"I'm not a fucking science experiment." Bryn put his shades on the table and both agents sucked in their breath.

"Woah."

"Yeah. You want me to show him these or not?"

"It might unsettle him," Gunnar said.

"We aim to try truth reading his answers to questions first. If that doesn't work, we'll ask you to describe his memories."

"According to Bryn, truth reading can be misleading," Gunnar said. "If the subject believes he's telling the truth, that's how it'll read. Right, Bryn?"

"Yeah. It's problematic with people with some psychological conditions. Split personalities, delusional schizophrenia..." Bryn went quiet as if recalling something unpleasant.

Gunnar flicked through the file again. "I guess we just get on with it. Bear in mind that Bryn isn't a psychic. This isn't hokum, it's a gene ability. He can't read this guy's mind and tell you what he's thinking in real time, it's about memory and intent."

"Noted." Agent Bell loosened his tie.

"And if Bryn wants out, that's what happens," Gunnar said, daring either of the agents to dispute it.

"Uh, Gunnar…" Bryn pulled on his sleeve. "You're getting wolfy."

Gunnar realized the rumbling growl he could hear was coming from his throat. *Hmm. That's new.*

Agent Gomez chuckled. "I heard wolves could be protective. We could do with a few more on our team. We have a bunch, but the cops steal too many of them."

Gunnar grunted. "Give me the address." Gomez sent it to Gunnar's cell. "We'll see you there." He ignored the agent's knowing smirk and marched from the room. *I need some bike time to clear my head. This gig is playing games with my Zen.* Bryn trailed after him. "They get you leathers and a helmet?"

"Yeah. Though apparently Warden was cursing a lot about how dangerous motorcycles are and that we should be using a nice, safe car with armored glass."

"Escaping a pursuer is easier on the bike. We can use a car if you want though." Gunnar gave himself a mental smack. *Should have asked what he wanted first. Idiot.*

"Hell no! I've seen your Harley, it's gorgeous."

"You ever been on a bike before?"

"No. I have a driver's license—I did driver's ed. in high school—but I haven't driven anything since, well, you know."

"Yeah. Right." Gunnar was beginning to realize that Bryn had been little more than a prisoner for the last three years. *No wonder he has a massive chip on his shoulder.*

Their gear was in a closet near the back entrance. Gunnar slung on his jacket and Bryn scrambled into a full body racing suit, which fitted over his clothes.

"Holy fuck!" Gunnar stroked the supple black leather. "This is high end. Has to be three thousand dollars' worth. Armored and...there's a built-in air bag. Of course there is."

"When you've finished drooling, you think you could help me with the helmet?"

"Sorry." Gunnar realized that Bryn's arm was in the sleeve he'd been fondling.

"I guess you don't need so much protection," Bryn said. "Lupines heal fast, don't they?"

"I don't mind wolf. Lupine is too scientific. We get damaged just as much as anyone else but yeah, we heal faster. Doesn't mean I ride like an idiot. I'll take care of you...Warden will have my balls if I don't, and I'm quite fond of them." Gunnar caught Bryn's blush before he rammed his helmet on his head. He helped him buckle it properly. "There, now all you have to do is hold on. Lean with my body. Okay?"

"Let's go." Bryn pulled on his gloves.

Riding the Harley, even in city traffic, always gave Gunnar a thrill. The experience improved tenfold with Bryn's arms wrapped around him. The FBI's Boston office in Chelsea was less than six miles away. On a good day the journey by car took fifteen minutes. On the bike, despite sections of gridlocked traffic, Gunnar did it in twelve.

When Bryn took off his helmet, his cheeks were flushed and his eyes even brighter than usual. He covered them with his shades. "That was fantastic! When can we do it again?"

Gunnar chuckled. "We have to get home, so that would be later today. Sadly we have work to do first."

"That sucks." Bryn unzipped his suit then struggled out of it. Gunnar stowed it and his jacket in the bike's panniers.

"Can't imagine anyone is going to steal it here." Gunnar noted that Bryn's posture had gone from relaxed to stiff at the mention of work. "You okay?"

"Yeah. No. I don't know. I haven't done this for a real case before. There's a lot riding on it and…it's not fun seeing this stuff."

"No, I don't imagine it is. If you need something else in your head when we're in there, you grab me. Okay?"

"You mean it?"

"Partners, remember."

"Okay. Stay within reach."

Gunnar led the way inside to where Agent Bell was waiting for them.

"You made good time. We left before you and only just got here."

"Get yourself a motorcycle, Agent. Though I know you guys are fond of the whole blacked-out windows thing."

"A hurtful stereotype, Detective. My personal transportation is a Prius." Bell sighed. "At my wife's insistence, I should make clear."

Bryn snorted with laughter and Gunnar grinned. They all needed a bit of a tension breaker.

"We're in the observation suite. Dr. Templeton is already situated. He's in cuffs, Bryn, which are anchored to the table. The only other person in the room will be his attorney, who has fewer morals than a timber rattler, and myself."

"I'll be there too," Gunnar said. "That's not negotiable."

"Of course. I should have made that clear. There will be other observers behind the glass. You've attracted a lot of interest."

"This isn't a freak show," Gunnar snapped.

"Not at all. Agents are lining up cases they think an augur can help them with. If this case can be closed because of Bryn, there'll be a line out the door."

"Can you point me at the bathroom?" Bryn asked.

Agent Bell pointed out the nearest facilities, just down the corridor. Bryn made a beeline for the door.

"Uh, excuse me a moment," Gunnar said. "I'm gonna go check on him." He followed Bryn. In the bathroom, puking sounds were coming from one of the stalls.

"Bryn, you need me to hold your hair back?"

There was a groan then the sound of flushing. Bryn emerged from the stall, pale, shoving his glasses back on his nose. He went to the sink and rinsed his mouth.

"Don't suppose you have a mint?"

"As it happens…" Gunnar extracted the remnants of a tube of Wint O Green Lifesavers from his pocket. "Take them. The mint will help settle your stomach."

Bryn shoved two candies in his mouth. "Don't tell Warden about this."

"About what? Your sensitive, sweet disposition?"

"Funny. Let's get this over with."

Gunnar had the good sense not to ask Bryn if he was sure. It wasn't like he had much choice.

Chapter Three

Why did he have to follow me into the bathroom? I'm quite capable of barfing on my own. Bryn washed his hands then put his gloves back on. *He must think I'm such a pathetic wuss. Which I am, apparently.* He couldn't get what the Forest Ripper had done out of his head. *If this is him, what am I going to see? Fuck. Someone needs to invent mind bleach.* He took a surreptitious glance at Gunnar. His expression didn't indicate anything other than professional stoicism. *He has to deal with this too, thanks to me.*

"You're gonna do fine." Gunnar followed Agent Bell through the building and Bryn scuffed along after him. "First time for anything is always the worst for nerves."

"I've never eaten sushi — pretty sure I'm not about to lose my breakfast before *that* new experience."

"I threw up the first time I went on a roller coaster," Gunnar said. "Humans, or wolves, were not designed to be upside down."

"So not the same! If I go green when we're in there, shoot me, okay?"

"Sure. I got ya."

They arrived at a nondescript door with the number eight on it. Bryn took a deep breath and schooled his features into a blank mask. *I can do this. Three years of crap has to be worth something.*

His first impression of Dr. Templeton was an anticlimax. He was dressed in prison orange and seated to one side of a table next to another man who had to be his attorney. Templeton was clean-shaven with short gray hair and a slightly hooked nose. *Not sure what I expected, but this wasn't it. He's so average. Apart from the eyes.* Bryn repressed a shudder. Templeton was staring at him and his dark eyes were cold, despite his fake smile.

Agent Bell took one of the free seats at the table then gestured for Bryn to join him. Gunnar lounged against the wall. Bryn wasn't fooled by his relaxed stance. He was alert and focused. Ready to move if he had to. It was reassuring. Bryn took the other chair.

"The augur will remove his glasses."

It was Templeton's attorney who spoke, though he didn't glance up from his notebook.

Bryn removed his shades, handing them to Gunnar. That made the attorney sit up and take notice.

"So he really is an augur," Templeton said. "Interesting."

"He is. Level five certified." Agent Bell sounded impatient. "As was confirmed to your counsel already."

"Forgive me for being skeptical," Templeton drawled. He rested his arms on the table, exposing the wrist cuffs.

"The augur will make contact with your skin. You'll then answer my questions and he'll read whether you are telling the truth or not."

Bryn stripped off his gloves. He rested his fingers across the underside of Templeton's wrist but the doctor grabbed his hand, squeezing it hard. Bryn closed his eyes. The pain helped him focus, something he didn't intend to reveal to anyone. A slight throb began at the base of his skull. He could sense Gunnar's rock-solid presence behind him and that eased his fear.

Agent Bell cleared his throat. "For the purposes of the recording, present in the room are..." He listed everyone by name. "Everard Templeton, did you murder Benny Solomon, aged seven, between July fifth and August twenty-ninth this year?"

"Oh, Agent, I don't think I'll be answering that question, or any others from you today." Templeton's tone was mocking.

"Truth," Bryn spoke softly.

"Very well." Agent Bell gave a pained sigh. "Subject is uncooperative. Bryn, if you would."

Bryn shifted his focus. It was hard to describe how his abilities worked, but he explained it as a switch. It wasn't anything physical but in his head he visualized a dial with three settings, one for detecting truth or lie, one to look into the past and another for the future. He could switch from one setting to another with a thought. For someone looking on, he appeared no different, though he had been told that sometimes his eyes flashed.

"What's going on?" Templeton's attorney was aggressive. Bryn tuned him out and went looking for Templeton's most powerful memory.

He saw hands. Hands around a slender neck, squeezing. A small scar on one finger. Whimpers. A sense of utter euphoria as a young life was extinguished. A child's face, tear-streaked. Sexual gratification.

Sickened, his head pounding, Bryn switched to the future.

A knife, the blade stained red. Bare skin. Myriad cuts. Black leather gloves discarded. His gloves.

"Fuck!" Bryn tore his hand free of Templeton's grasp. Blindly he reached for Gunnar, grabbed his wrist, and he saw a winding road, the sea, felt exhilaration and freedom. Bryn took long, slow breaths and opened his eyes. Templeton's hands were flat on the table, the scar on one finger clearly visible. He was smirking.

"He enjoyed it. Got off on it." Bryn shoved his chair back and stood so he could get closer to Gunnar. "Torture then slow strangulation. I can identify the victim. I saw the child's face." He realized he was still clutching Gunnar's wrist and let go.

"Would he kill again if he were free to?" Agent Bell asked.

"Yes." Bryn didn't elaborate.

Templeton's attorney's face was an interesting shade of purple. He was visibly sweating. "You can't use any of that."

"We can and you know it." Agent Bell slapped his hand down on the table. "Your client is going away for a very long time. He's lucky Massachusetts has no death penalty."

Gunnar handed Bryn his shades and it was a relief to hide behind the dark lenses. He pulled on his gloves and tried to signal to Gunnar that he needed to get out of the room. Templeton's gazed was pinned on him and his hatred was palpable. Bryn had absolutely no doubt that Templeton would kill him if he could and it would be a slow, painful death of a thousand cuts.

"You need us in here any longer, Bell?" Gunnar asked.

"No. You can both go. Stick around outside, though."

Gunnar was already at the door and Bryn was right behind him. In the corridor he could breathe. Gunnar squeezed his shoulder. "How are you doing? You need a bucket?"

Bryn snorted. "I appreciate the thought, but no. Head hurts. Can we get some water?"

"Sure. We can wait in the lobby. I spotted a vending machine when we came in. Agent Bell will find us when he needs to."

Gunnar guided Bryn to the lobby and left him on a couch while he raided the vending machine. He returned with a cold bottle of water and some candy bars. "Thought you could use the sugar too. I also have Tylenol." He popped two pills from a packet and handed them over. He also unscrewed the bottle cap. "That was rough, huh? That guy gave me the creeps."

"He enjoyed what he did, Gunnar. Loved it. Those poor fucking kids."

"And he'd have carried on doing it if not for you. Did you look at his future?"

"I'd seen enough. Him cutting flesh. Blood rising from the wounds."

"Fuck."

"Yeah." Bryn swallowed more water.

"Sick fucker." Gunnar unwrapped a candy bar then shoved half of it in his mouth.

"I reckon he thinks he's still going to be released. He's deluded. Gimme my candy."

"You want to touch him again, take a look at his future intent?"

"I'd rather stick my hand in a nest of tarantulas." Bryn chomped the candy in three bites. "I couldn't have done that without you."

"I didn't do anything. I just stood there. Wanted to rip the guy's head off, so go me for restraint."

"You made me feel safe," Bryn muttered. "Fuck, my head hurts." He took his shades off then knuckled his eyes. "On a scale of cat to freaky alien, where am I?"

"Oh, you're up there with ET at the moment."

"Frig." Bryn slammed his shades back on.

"What did you see when you touched me?" Gunnar asked.

"We were on the bike together, on the open road somewhere. Freedom."

"When we're done here, I'm going to take you on a ride out to the coast. Get some sea air into your lungs and lobster in your belly. First job together needs celebrating."

"That sounds..." *Perfect.* "Warden will never allow it."

"Who said anything about asking?" Gunnar grinned. "Don't look now, but Special Agent Bell is approaching. He seems animated."

"Is it too late to make a run for it?"

"Not a hope."

"I thought I'd lost you two!" Agent Bell beamed. "The doctor is safely locked away. His attorney is still spluttering and making empty threats. We need to go upstairs for a debrief."

"Sure thing." Gunnar grabbed Bryn's arm and pulled him to his feet. "Let's get this done."

"Bryn, I can't tell you...*you* are a walking miracle. There are a lot of people keen to meet you."

"Oh God." Bryn looked for the nearest fire exit sign.

"Oh no you don't." Gunnar gave him a disapproving glance. "Don't need to be an augur to know what you're planning, sunshine."

"Spoilsport."

"Yeah, yeah. I exist to rain on your parade. Play nice with the federal agents or you'll end up in some black site a mile underground."

"Been there, done that," Bryn muttered. "Didn't even get a T-shirt."

Gunnar stared at him. "You and I really need to get to know each other better."

"You weren't meant to hear that."

"Wolf, remember? I can hear a bunny sneeze across six miles of forest."

"Useful skill." Bryn was glad Gunnar couldn't see him rolling his eyes behind his dark glasses.

"Roll those eyes any harder and they'll fall out."

Damn it!

"How long have you two been partners?" Agent Bell asked.

"A day," Gunnar said.

"No way. You act like an old married couple."

To Bryn's relief, they arrived at Bell's office, which was the base for the team of agents investigating the Forest Ripper case. As they went in, they got a round of applause. Bryn edged behind Gunnar. Agent Bell waved his colleagues away. "Come sit down. You want coffee?"

"God, yes." Bryn slumped into a chair and tried to ignore the curious looks cast his way from around the room. "Black. Please."

"Cream, three sugars," Gunnar chimed in. "Where's your partner?"

"Food poisoning. He's gone home." Bell sent a junior agent for coffee then opened his laptop. "Everything from the interview with Dr. Templeton was recorded, but I need to make some notes about what you saw, Bryn. We need to confirm which of the victims you observed and anything else worth noting."

"Okay." Bryn didn't want to relive the experience but this was an essential part of the process. "If every suspect refuses to answer questions while I'm in contact, that's going to be a problem, isn't it?"

"They won't all be as sharp as Templeton," Gunnar said. "Some won't believe you can do anything at all and they'll treat it like a challenge. Some will think they can fool you by thinking of other things. They won't understand that you're not reading their minds."

"I concur, Detective. Your skills will be useful for testing the veracity of witnesses too, Bryn. That could be revealing, and they won't have grounds to refuse truth reading." He tapped on his keyboard. "Okay, describe exactly what you saw."

Bryn closed his eyes then went over everything he'd observed from Templeton's strongest memory.

"And you're sure he got off on it?" Bell asked.

"Definitely."

"Must have worn a rubber. No trace of semen on any of the bodies. Was there anything specific that confirms he was the active participant and not observing someone else?"

"Other than his emotions, there was the scar on his third finger, from nail to knuckle. It was distinctive. I didn't see his face. No reflective surfaces."

"Okay. For the record, can you tell the difference between participation and observation?"

"Yes. All confirmed in my testing record." Bryn shifted. "You want me to identify which victim was involved?"

"Yeah. Their pictures are on the board over there." Agent Bell pointed at a whiteboard in one corner of the room. Twelve photographs formed a line across the top.

Someone handed Bryn a cup of coffee and he walked across the room. He avoided reading the notes and focused on the young faces. "It was him." He indicated the eighth victim. "I wonder what was different about him." He turned away from the board.

Gunnar was reading the notes on the board. "He was the son of a woman who rejected Templeton. A nurse at the hospital. Widowed. Jesus." He growled and a couple of agents in the room joined in. "Wolves know true evil."

Bryn went back to Bell's desk. "Is there an entire pack in here?"

Bell grinned. "Only two. When they get to growling, you'd think there were more and I wish there were. Wolves are perfect for law enforcement." He tapped his pen against his lips. "Do you think I'd stand any chance at all of getting you two attached here permanently?"

Bryn shrugged. "Those decisions are way above my pay grade."

"You'd have to get in touch with Warden," Gunnar said, "but I don't like your chances."

"No, me either." Bell frowned. "I'll pull together a priority list of cases you could help with anyway. Has to be worth a shot."

"Are you done with us for now?"

"Sure," Bell said, pushing his chair back to stand. He shook Gunnar's hand then gave Bryn a suspicious look.

"It's okay, the gloves are on for a reason." Bryn shook his hand too.

"I hope it's not the last we see of you both. It shouldn't be long before Templeton appears in court. He'll be forced to plead guilty to the murder you saw, Bryn. Hopefully his arrogance will have him pleading the same for the rest. It'll be life regardless. Even the most liberal judges don't go easy on child killers."

Bryn nodded. "I hope he spends a long time in a very unpleasant place." He headed for the door, hoping Gunnar was following. He wanted out of the building and some distance between him and Templeton, even if the man was safely locked away. "Are we really going to go for a ride?"

"Sure are. I don't know about you, but I need some clean sea air in my lungs."

Zipping himself into black leather was a way of hiding. With his helmet on no one could see Bryn's expression. There were things in his head he could never unsee and he had to find a way of dealing with it. *One case and I'm already a mess. This job is going to kill me.* He straddled the bike behind Gunnar then wrapped his arms around Gunnar's waist. His solid torso was an anchor.

"Just hold on. You don't have to do anything else," Gunnar said through the helmet intercom. "I'm going to head for Yirrell Beach in Winthrop. It's not too far for your first trip."

Gunnar didn't say anything else and Bryn switched off. He focused on the power and speed of the bike, the throb of the engine and swaying with Gunnar's body as he took bends. He was sad when the short trip ended. There was a parking lot right next to the beach and it wasn't too busy. Gunnar locked their leathers in the panniers.

"How was that?" Gunnar asked.

"Not far enough," Bryn said. "But it feels great to be away from Warden and out of the city."

"Another time we'll go farther. When we have a day off."

"So why here?"

"I like watching the 'planes coming in and out of the airport," Gunnar said. "Also, there's a place on Main

Street that does the best lobster rolls in the area." He patted his stomach.

"Are you ever not hungry?" Bryn wasn't sure he could face eating anything just yet.

"Nope. Wolf metabolism needs fuel." Gunnar stretched. "You want to walk a ways?" A buzzing sounded from his pocket and he pulled out his cell. "Warden. Took him longer than I thought it would. Hey, boss."

Bryn waited for the inevitable explosion. Gunnar held the phone away from his ear. "Yes, boss, we are at the beach. No, I haven't lost him. No, he's nowhere near a boat or seagoing vessel of any kind." *What the fuck?* he mouthed at Bryn. "It's called aftercare, sir. No, not that kind of aftercare, and why would you know about that anyway? No, none of my business. I'll have him back by ten. Yes, boss, they do have the best lobster rolls." Gunnar ended the call then stared at the cell as if he couldn't believe what he just heard.

Bryn scuffed his boot on the asphalt. "Tell me I didn't just learn that my boss is into kink."

"I'm not gonna start lying to you now, Bryn, but fuck...sometimes there are things I don't want to be visualizing."

"Tell me about it." Bryn met Gunnar's eyes and they both dissolved into laughter. "Gives me an alternative to what I saw earlier. They always say imagine your audience naked, but this tops that by a mile."

"Tops it...?" Gunnar guffawed.

"Oh my God, juvenile much? I thought I was the immature half of this partnership." Bryn felt the most relaxed he'd been all day.

"Come on. We'll walk down the beach and find a bench. Then you can talk about your feelings and shit."

"Fuck off."

Gunnar chuckled. "And the brat is back. You're gonna be fine."

Chapter Four

The following morning, Bryn dragged himself into the kitchen after a poor night's sleep. *I need sugar in the worst way.* It was only when he opened the cupboard that he remembered the cereal situation. "I am not eating that shredded cardboard."

"And you don't have to." Gunnar came into the kitchen fresh from the shower and smelling of freshly cut grass, his long hair still damp. He put a box of frosted flakes on the counter. "I got these when I went out for a run earlier. But, if you want to avoid a diabetic coma, I made something last night."

"You've been out running. What is wrong with you?"

"Wolves like to run."

"Don't think I'm going with you. Early mornings are to be spent under a warm comforter, not pounding the sidewalks. What did you make?"

Gunnar went to the fridge and pulled out two dishes. "Fruit compote on the bottom, then a layer of thick Greek yogurt, then granola on the top. Try it."

Bryn eyed the dish with suspicion. "It sounds healthy."

"That's the general idea. If you don't like it, you can eat the sugar-death, okay?"

"Fine. Need coffee, though."

"I unpacked my French press last night when you were catching up on your beauty sleep. Sit. Eat. I'll make coffee."

"You know I'm all grown up, don't you?" Bryn sat at the table and pulled one of the bowls toward him. "I can look after myself."

"Debatable, at least before coffee."

Bryn scowled but dug in to his breakfast. "Oh wow, this is good!"

"I know, genius. I'm making eggs too." Gunnar bustled away chopping, beating and stirring and after a while served up scrambled eggs, wholewheat toast and coffee.

"I could get used to this." Bryn ate every scrap and drank two cups of excellent coffee.

"We can take it in turns," Gunnar said, finishing his own meal. "If you don't know how, I'll teach you."

"Cooking lessons. Yay." *Actually that sounds kind of fun.* "What delights has Warden got in store for us today?"

Gunnar checked his cell. "A visit to MCI Cedar Junction. An interesting one, this. There's a guy in there who has consistently protested his innocence, name of Dwayne Scott. Not unusual, but his case is one that was investigated by a corrupt cop."

"So I get to find out if he's innocent or guilty?"

"Yeah. The full file is in the conference room waiting for us."

"If this guy is innocent, it'll make a change from all the sewer-level memories I've seen over the last three years. It would really be doing something good."

"I guess your training wasn't a picnic?" Gunnar crunched a piece of charred toast.

Bryn stared at him. "Wolves need charcoal?"

"Hey, no judging. I like it crispy."

"Hmm and no, it wasn't."

"When you're ready, you can tell me about it. Might be therapeutic."

"Therapists run screaming from the room where I'm concerned, believe me. Tell me about the federal pen. Doesn't it take a while to get clearance to go in there?"

"Yeah. I've done a few visits. We have to comply with BOP policies."

"Bop?"

"Bureau of Prisons. So I guess Warden has already been on the case because approval for the visit has to be requested. That usually means contacting the prison where the inmate is housed and explaining the purpose of the visit, so that must have been fun."

"No kidding."

"So then a visit is scheduled and the prison will arrange for necessary security measures based on the nature of the visit and the inmate's status."

"Like what?"

"Additional guards, that kind of thing. Then when we get there, we check in at the visitor entrance and go through security screening. I'll probably have to leave my gun. Then we'll have an escort to the designated meeting area, most likely a secure interview room. Then you do your thing."

"You make it sound so easy." Bryn scowled. "Will there be people watching?"

"I guess the inmate's legal representative may be there, and someone from the prison. I've not been in this exact situation before, remember?"

"Are we taking the bike?"

"Not today. I want to stop by the store on the way back and pick up some provisions."

"Yeah?" Bryn's mood lightened. "Can I pick out stuff I like?"

"Sure. We have a decent budget from Warden."

"Good. I need Twinkies."

"Of course you do."

"Chocolate cream or mixed berry."

"Not vanilla?" Gunnar gave him a sly grin.

"Really? You're going there?"

"A totally innocent inquiry, Bryn. What were *you* thinking about?"

"Fuck off."

"Aw, are you blushing?"

"Two days. We've been partners for two days and I already want to kill you."

"Heh. You lasted two days longer than my first partner. He wanted my head on a plate minutes after he walked through the door. He mistook my sniffing him as something sexual. Never could convince him it wasn't."

"Especially when it was?"

"Well, yeah. There is that. You love me really. Get your ass in gear, we need to go. I'll meet you downstairs."

Bryn watched him go. "That man has far too much energy for this time of day. Running. Ugh." He walked through to his bathroom. *I wonder what products he uses on that mop of his and...what the actual fuck am I thinking about that for?* He cleaned his teeth before risking a glance in the mirror. His eyes weren't too eerie yet—they were always dimmest after a night's sleep and brightest after he'd been using his abilities. All attempts at learning ways of dialing down the glow had so far failed. He grabbed his gloves and a jacket from his bedroom and put on his sunglasses. *Better go earn the right to keep on breathing, I guess.*

Gunnar was waiting outside the conference room door. He thrust a folder at Bryn. "Here. You can read it in the car. Do you own any clothing that isn't black?"

"No." Bryn scowled. "How much plaid flannel is there in *your* closet?" He followed Gunnar outside, noting how his broad shoulders barely fit through the doorway. *Stop riling the man who could bench press your skinny self, Bryn, you dumbass.*

"No dissing the flannel. It's soft and warm. I like it for the same reason I prefer beaten up Levi's. Comfort and practicality."

"How old are you? Fifty?"

"Twenty-seven, you cheeky brat." Gunnar opened the gate. A black Taurus was parked in the alley.

"Oh my God, could they have picked a more stereotypical vehicle?" Bryn scrambled into the passenger seat.

"You want to drive?" Gunnar dangled the key from a finger.

"You mean it?"

"Sure. Gimme the file back. I'll read you the good bits."

Bryn grabbed the key before Gunnar could change his mind. He ran around to the driver's seat. "It's been a while."

"Not my car, is it? You need to get familiar. If there's ever a situation when I'm down and you need to get away, you have to be able to drive confidently. Besides, it's an automatic. Not much to it. Personally, I prefer a stick."

Bryn didn't want to imagine a time when he'd have to abandon his partner, however annoying he was. He got behind the wheel then buckled up. The in-built sat-nav was programmed for the penitentiary, so all he had to do was follow directions. He set off and the exhilaration of being in charge of his own destination was heady. *I could keep driving. Go for miles. What could they do?*

"Keep your eyes on the road and your hands on the wheel. I might only be a wolf but it doesn't take a genius to guess what's going through your head right now."

"Don't know what you mean."

"Yeah, right. You have a tracker chip in you and I don't want to be involved in a pursuit with the cops on our second case."

"Spoilsport."

"Behave or I won't let you drive again."

"This isn't a one-off?"

"If you get us there in one piece."

Bryn tightened his grip on the steering wheel. He kept quiet for the rest of the journey and listened to Gunnar as he read out some background from the file.

"So this guy went down for armed robbery?"

"Yeah. He had some financial issues then seemed to be cash rich, which is why he attracted attention. He was in the neighborhood and his car was caught on camera on the same road as the convenience store that was robbed."

"But no positive ID?"

"Perp wore a clown mask. The store owner, assistant and two customers were gunned down."

"So no witnesses?"

"It happened at night. One witness saw a masked man run past him on the sidewalk. He testified to height, build and a tattoo on the perp's neck. An anchor."

"He saw a tat, in the dark, on a running man?"

"Yeah. Kinda sketchy. Witness has since died so can't be questioned. The arresting cop has been fired and is being prosecuted for, amongst other things, taking bribes from organized crime gangs, excessive force, racist language…the list goes on."

"Sounds like a charmer."

"A charmer who could have mentioned that tat to the witness."

"How long has the guy we're seeing been locked up?"

"Five years."

"Fuck."

"Don't make any assumptions."

"What I think makes zero difference to the outcome."

"You can't lie about what you see?"

"No. If I try it, something in my brain short circuits. The pain is so bad I black out."

"Do I want to know how that was discovered?"

"No. You really don't." Bryn sighed. "You know what a shock collar is?"

"I do."

"When you're told to lie or be shocked, you lie, especially when the interrogator already knows the answer to the questions. The subject is asked something obvious like, is your dog's name Fido? The subject says yes because that is the dog's name but I'm instructed to say he's lying. Carry out the experiment a hundred times for avoidance of doubt. Case proven."

"Fuck."

"That's one way of putting it. Eventually the shocks were the better option. Damned if you do, damned if you don't."

"That's all kinds of wrong."

"Yeah, well…" Bryn pulled into the prison visitors' lot.

"Nice driving. Didn't have to grab the 'oh shit' handle once." Gunnar got out of the Taurus, grinning.

"So I can drive back?"

"Let's see how you feel after you've done your thing."

Bryn scowled his way through the prison security checks. The place was claustrophobic and brought back memories he'd rather have avoided. The interview room was gray and windowless. There was no two-way viewing facility like at the FBI and the whole place had an air of neglect. The overpowering smell was of disinfectant.

"This place could use an interior designer." Bryn slumped in an uncomfortable metal chair on one side of a table, which was bolted to the floor. "Maybe a rug. Some artwork."

"It's okay to be nervous." Gunnar seemed relaxed but a slight tension around the eyes betrayed him.

"I'm not. The sooner we get started the sooner you take me shopping for Twinkies."

Gunnar shook his head. "Where's our customer?"

Bryn stripped off his gloves and removed his shades. He handed both to Gunnar. "May as well give him the freaky eyes from the start."

"Next time you call yourself a freak, I'm gonna put you over my…" Gunnar clamped his mouth shut as the door opened.

"Yeah, hold that thought."

The inmate that came into the room escorted by a corrections officer was dressed in prison garb. The exposed parts of his arms were covered with tattoos. His hair was shaved close to his skull and there was some faded bruising around one eye. He was even bigger than Gunnar.

Gunnar sniffed. "Wolf."

Bryn eyed the man who took the chair opposite him. "You have counsel, Mr. Scott?"

"Nah. What the fuck are you, pretty boy?"

"Your way outta here if you're telling the truth, so be nice." Bryn folded his arms across his chest. "Why hasn't he been told what's happening?"

The CO leaned in. "We're short-staffed. His brief couldn't get here but the superintendent is joining us."

Gunnar grunted. "Fine. While we're waiting then, Mr. Scott, Bryn is an augur. Your conviction is being questioned because the arresting officer was corrupt…"

"That fucker should be in here, not me."

"That's what we're here to determine. Do you know what an augur can do?"

"How the fuck should I know?"

"He'll know whether or not you're telling the truth."

"You're shitting me?"

"I shit you not." Gunnar scowled. "You willing to go through with it?"

"Too fucking right I am. You really mean it?" Scott's tone got softer.

"He's a wolf. He isn't going to lie to you," Bryn said.

It was a few more minutes before they were joined by the superintendent, who seemed harried to the point of an impending nervous breakdown. When he spoke, his accent was all Georgia peaches and cream.

"Gentlemen, I apologize for keeping you waiting. Shall we get this show the road?"

"I need skin-to-skin contact, Mr. Scott." Bryn held out his hand. Scott grabbed it, the strength of his grip making Bryn wince.

"Ease off, Dwayne," Gunnar said. "He doesn't need broken fingers."

Bryn gave him a grateful glance and shifted his grip to Dwayne's wrist before closing his eyes for focus. He gave the briefest of nods.

"Dwayne Scott, on September fifteenth, five years ago, were you in the vicinity of the 7-Eleven on Berkeley?" Gunnar asked.

"Yeah, I was. Had to pick up some meds from the late-night pharmacy."

"Truth," Bryn confirmed.

"Did you enter the 7-Eleven with the intention of robbing the store?"

"No. Didn't go in there."

"Truth."

"Were you armed that night?"

"No."

"Truth."

"Have you ever knowingly committed a crime?" Gunnar asked.

"Shit, man...I maybe smoked some weed a few years back."

"Truth."

"You deal?"

"Fuck no. I ain't into no shit like that."

"Truth."

"Okay, Bryn is going to look at your memories now."

Bryn changed his focus. "Cute kid. He's holding a baby, saying well done to a woman in the hospital."

"My boy. He's almost six now." Scott's voice trembled. "I won't let his momma bring him here. She's stuck by me, though."

"Future intent then, Bryn."

"Hugging his kid. Taking him to the park. Going bowling…"

"Okay, I think we're done here. Superintendent, you have any more questions you need answered?"

"No. It seems that a grave miscarriage of justice has occurred. I'll expedite Mr. Scott's release as soon as possible."

"That's it?" Dwayne Scott gaped. Bryn let go of his arm and massaged his temples.

"That's it. There's no disputing the word of a certified augur," Gunnar said. He handed Bryn his gloves and glasses. "Good luck, Dwayne."

"Thanks, man. When I'm out, you ever need anything, you come find me."

"Have a great life." Gunnar squeezed Bryn's shoulder. "How you doing?"

"Not too bad. Feels like we did something good." He pushed his chair back. The CO left with Scott but the superintendent closed the door behind them.

"This is not an authorized request, but I'd like to ask you guys a favor."

Gunnar frowned but Bryn shrugged. "Go ahead."

"The reason we're having staffing problems today…bordering on a riot situation…is an accusation from an inmate about one of the corrections officers."

"What's the accusation?" Gunnar asked.

"Rape. Inmate says the officer assaulted him in his cell. There are no witnesses so it's his word against the CO's."

"What does the CO say?"

"That it's a pile of horseshit. One more scumbag trying to get him in trouble."

"You disagree?"

"I know better than to take one side or the other without evidence, but the unrest is about to blow up. Bryn here could throw ice water on the fire."

"This ain't like shelling peas. It takes a lot out of him," Gunnar said.

"Hey...we're already here." Bryn tilted his head from side to side, wincing at the cracking sounds. "How do you want to do this?"

"My office. Simpler to question the officer than the inmate. He's an employee so he doesn't get to say no. Inmate could refuse unless his lawyer was present."

"You sure about this, Bryn? I don't want your head to explode or anything." Gunnar wrinkled his nose. "Warden would end me himself."

"My brain is not going to explode." *Don't think I'll be driving anywhere later, but what the heck.* "I think we should do it."

"Okay." Gunnar didn't look happy.

Fuck, he's sexy when he gets all growly. Stop thinking like that, idiot. He's your work partner, nothing more. Bryn trailed after the superintendent and Gunnar, making a conscious effort not to wince at every clanging door or loud noise. The superintendent's office proved to be a quiet sanctuary. It was utilitarian and as gray as everywhere else in the prison but had to have some kind of sound proofing to deaden the noise from outside. After the super made a quick call on an old-fashioned desk phone, they waited. Gunnar paced and Bryn lounged on a windowsill. The bars didn't enhance the view but at least the window was high enough that the sky was visible above the prison walls.

"When Officer Phelps arrives, I'll ask him straight out if the rape allegations are true," the superintendent said. "We'll get this over with quickly."

"Will he be carrying?" Gunnar asked. "Because he won't react well if he's lying."

"No. Basic officers inside the penitentiary don't carry firearms. He carries pepper spray. He is qualified to carry firearms so has the magazine pouches and holster rigs on his duty belt, but they are only issued a holster and weapon for transports outside the pen or for specific posts on areas like the perimeter or lobby."

Gunnar grunted. "Wonderful. Bryn, you watch yourself."

"Isn't that your job?" Bryn briefly lifted his glasses and batted his lashes at his partner, knowing it would annoy the hell out of him.

"Try to remember which one of us is in charge."

"Exactly."

"I don't get paid nearly enough for this gig," Gunnar grumbled. He went to stand by the door.

Bryn took his gloves off and tucked them into his waistband. He kept his glasses on. The superintendent took a seat behind his desk but stood when Officer Phelps arrived. Bryn took an instant dislike to the officer, who oozed arrogance. He had a paunch, pallid skin and cruel eyes.

"Officer Phelps, you're aware we've had a complaint against you?" The superintendent didn't waste any time with preliminaries.

"Wouldn't be a day with a y in it if there hadn't been. Cons got nothing better to do than make shit up."

The super gave a non-committal grunt. "Well, we are fortunate to be able to clear this up quickly. I'd like to introduce you to Bryn Ashton. He's an augur."

Phelps' face reddened. "The fuck he is."

"He was here helping with another case but kindly offered to stay so that we could remove all doubt about your situation as quickly as possible. This isn't an accusation you need hanging over you."

Bryn took off his glasses and grinned at Phelps' wince. On this occasion, he was happy his eyes made someone uncomfortable. "Give me your hand." He held out his own.

"Why?"

"I need skin-to-skin contact for this to work." Bryn held down a shudder when Phelps took his hand. His palm was sweaty and he gripped too hard for comfort, but Bryn had been trained not to show any emotion. He pressed his thumb to the underside of Phelps' wrist. "I'm ready."

"Did you assault prisoner Da Costa? You only need answer yes or no."

"No." Phelps' word was accompanied by a spray of spittle.

"Lie." Bryn locked on to Phelps' memory. "He's done it before too." He yanked his hand away but Phelps grabbed him and got an arm around Bryn's throat. He pulled a knife, but Gunnar was far too quick for him. He dragged Bryn away and disarmed Phelps in one swift movement. He had Phelps on the floor with a knee in his back seconds later.

"Where the fuck did this lowlife get a knife?"

Bryn backed away. He really wanted to wash his hands. The super was white-faced and already making a call for backup, which arrived seconds later. Two uniformed men crashed through the office door, guns raised.

"What did you see, Bryn?" Gunnar asked.

"He was raping a man. Ginger hair, freckles, looked young. He was enjoying it. The power as much as the act. He called him Jimmy, so I knew it was someone different from the accuser."

"Jimmy Allen, killed himself in his cell. Get this garbage out of my office," the superintendent snapped. "Read him his rights then put him in a holding cell. Maybe he'll get lucky and be sent back here in a different colored uniform. That would be justice."

Gunnar dragged Phelps to his feet then pushed him at the armed officers. "He's all yours."

"Nicely done, Detective."

"He was predictable and dumb as a rock." Gunnar put the knife on the super's desk.

"And evil," Bryn contributed. "It wouldn't surprise me if you get a lot more inmates coming forward after this. I'd guess he's been abusing his position for a long time."

"It's sickening. The COs wear body cams but it's too easy to obscure the footage or claim the camera isn't working. I can only thank you for helping, but I'll be sending a report to your superiors. This has been invaluable and I hope we can work together again, particularly if it means freeing more people who've suffered injustices."

Gunnar shook the super's hand but Bryn just nodded as he put his dark glasses on. He couldn't wait to leave the cloying prison atmosphere and breathe fresh air.

Chapter Five

"You look like a two-day-old corpse," Gunnar said as he and Bryn made their way out of the prison to the parking lot. He was worried Bryn had done too much.

"Well thanks." Bryn massaged his neck. "That boosts my self-esteem no end."

"You did a great job in there but you shouldn't overdo it." Gunnar opened the car door and hoisted Bryn into the passenger seat before he could protest. It was worrying that Bryn didn't say anything sarcastic or gripe about being manhandled. "Maybe we should head back to the apartment?" Gunnar said as he got behind the wheel.

"No way. You are not getting out of buying me Twinkies. I want my trip to the market. Chemically enhanced goodness will make me feel so much better."

"You know that's not a good thing, right?"

"Drive, wolf boy. We can get you some goodies too." Bryn slumped in his seat and Gunnar guessed that his eyes were closed behind his glasses.

"Okay, but you ain't gonna fit in the kiddie seat in the cart. You'll have to walk."

"Fuck off."

Gunnar grinned — that was the spark of attitude he'd been looking for.

There was a Walmart less than fifteen minutes' drive away so Gunnar headed there. He hoped it wouldn't be too crowded but if Bryn pushed the cart, he'd have a bit of protection. When they got there, the lot was more than half full. Bryn's face was still bone white, accentuated by his dark clothing and hair, and Gunnar was a bit concerned about how he'd cope being around so many people. *Not going to insult him by asking if he's sure about this. The kid knows his own mind even if his decisions aren't always in his best interests.*

"We're here."

Bryn perked up. "You know how long it's been since I had free rein in one of these places? Never. The group home was always on a budget and once I went into training, I didn't get any choice about what I ate."

"This may be the first time but it won't be the last, so go easy. I don't need you bouncing off the walls because you've eaten a shit-ton of candy."

"I need chips and strawberries and chicken tenders and stuff to make sliders and..."

"Shall we get in there?" Gunnar chuckled. "I get the feeling this is going to be an expensive trip."

"It's Warden's dollar." Bryn shrugged. "He can afford it."

In the end it was Gunnar who pushed the cart because Bryn kept getting distracted and running off to different shelves. He drew a few curious looks but Walmart's clientele was the full spectrum of humanity. There were shoppers who looked a lot stranger than Bryn.

Bryn had apparently found his Nirvana. Even though he did pick out a lot of sweet, unhealthy things, he also stocked the cart with the makings of lots of different dishes.

"We can have mac and cheese tonight, can't we? With garlic bread? I even got salad for you."

"I love homemade mac and cheese," Gunnar admitted, licking his lips.

"I hope you know how to cook it, because I don't have a clue," Bryn said.

"As it happens, I do." Gunnar eyed the heaped cart. "I think it's time I got you out of here or there won't be any groceries left for anyone else."

"Okay, deal. Can we make a stop at a Walgreens? I think I'm going to need a fresh supply of painkillers."

"Don't worry about that. Warden has it covered. You'll be able to get what you need back at base. Prescription strength rather than over-the-counter meds."

"Good to know Warden has a candy store just for me," Bryn muttered.

There was a line at the checkouts and while Gunnar waited, Bryn wandered off to browse the chips aisle for a second time. When he came back, Gunnar was paying and Bryn had to negotiate his way through the line. "Sorry, sorry... Coming through. I'm with the big guy."

It was impossible for him not to brush past people and Gunnar suddenly realized that Bryn hadn't put his gloves back on. Their eyes met and Gunnar knew that Bryn had connected with someone and whatever he'd seen hadn't been good. He looked shell-shocked. There were so many people there was no way of telling who it had been. Bryn stumbled toward the exit and Gunnar followed him shoving the cart like a battering ram. Shoppers scattered and they made it outside.

"Hold the side of the cart. You look like you're about to fall over."

Bryn grabbed it but still weaved as he walked. Gunnar had parked in an empty portion of the lot. He shoved bags of groceries into the trunk as fast as he could then got Bryn into the car before abandoning the cart and getting in himself.

"Tell me."

"I'm so dumb. I should have known better."

"It's not your fault… What did you see?"

"Not sure if it was memory or the future. Death. So much death." Bryn slumped and Gunnar realized he'd lost consciousness. He checked his pulse and that he was breathing easily then reclined his seat before buckling him in. He called Warden to let him know what was going on and that they were on their way back. Warden assured him that he'd be waiting with medical personnel. Gunnar drove as fast as he could, glancing at his partner every few seconds.

Warden was as good as his word and as soon as Gunnar pulled up outside the GCR HQ, Bryn was efficiently extracted from the car and carried into the property. Warden instructed one of his staff to unload Gunnar's groceries while they went inside for a debrief. They settled into the conference room and within minutes, coffee and a plate of pastries had arrived. Gunnar couldn't help but admire Warden's ruthless efficiency.

"Take me through the day from the beginning, Detective. Don't leave anything out."

Gunnar took his time, taking Warden through first the case he and Bryn had been assigned, then the favor they'd done for the prison superintendent. Warden didn't say a word, though his expression spoke volumes. Gunnar finished by describing the trip to the store, Bryn's excitement and then what had apparently happened at the checkout line.

"And after I got him into the car, I called you and the rest you know."

Warden poured them both a coffee. "I think we need this."

"The super kinda hijacked us at the prison," Gunnar said. "I wasn't happy about Bryn doing another job so quickly but he insisted he was okay."

"Bryn knows his limitations, Gunnar, and believe me I know how difficult it is to convince him not to do something he's already set his mind on. Stubborn doesn't begin to describe him. I've met less obstinate granite boulders."

"For him, it's a strength."

"I agree. It's unlikely he would have survived his training if he was weaker. That doesn't make him infallible, nor does it make him Superman. Doing what he does has significant physical consequences. He doesn't want to accept that, but it's the truth. I think, on this occasion, you were right to let him carry on. I will, however, be writing to the prison superintendent to express my disappointment that he didn't follow correct channels in requesting our assistance."

Gunnar decided he was glad he wasn't going to be on the receiving end of that email. "But what about the market? I should have made sure he was wearing his gloves."

"That's his responsibility, not yours. You're not his babysitter, you're his partner, though inevitably keeping him safe is going to be part of your job."

"His head hurt but he was excited about going to the store. He was distracted and I should have reminded him. I didn't even notice and that's on me. That contact must have been one too many."

"It's only been two days, so let's mark it down to experience. I'm sure it won't happen again. Did you see anything that made you suspicious about the people in that line?"

Gunnar shook his head. "I had my card out, I was paying... I didn't take any notice of the people in the line behind me. There weren't enough staff on the checkouts, so even though the store wasn't that crowded, there were lots of people in line, jostling and impatient. When Bryn came to join me, he had to push his way through maybe a dozen or more people. I don't think he'll know who it was he touched that triggered such a strong reaction."

"Well, we'll see. We can debrief him together once he's rested and been cleared by the doctor."

"Yeah, I guess he needs to sleep a while."

"Word about you two is already getting around. I knew we wouldn't be able to keep him a secret, but law enforcement is a small community and the worst for gossip. You would not believe the number of requests I've already had for your services."

"Fuck, we'll have to be careful he doesn't burn out."

"Yes, we certainly will. What happened today might actually play in our favor, strange as it seems. All right, you've had a long day too. Write up your report then we'll reconvene once Bryn is fit to talk, probably in the morning."

As Gunnar climbed the stairs to the apartment, he mused on Warden's reactions. He'd expected a much harsher dressing down but Warden had been fair.

Maybe he's not so bad after all. Shit, this gig will either kill me or make me. The kid is going to give me gray hairs. Except he isn't a kid at all. He loosened his bun and shook it out. "First stop, shower. Second… Think I need to steal a Twinkie."

When he got to the apartment, the doctor was just leaving. "Detective, we put Bryn in his own bed, there's no need for a hospital. I've given him a sedative and some stronger pain meds so he'll be out for a while. He needs rest more than anything."

"Okay, tell me, Doc, these headaches he gets, are they dangerous?"

"We've been scanning his brain every month for several years now and there's no sign of any damage. Think of it as muscle strain. You chase down a criminal and maybe your hamstring aches or you get a sore knee. What Bryn does utilizes parts of his brain that we have very little understanding of. If he does too much it's like a muscle strain, but a hell of a lot more painful."

"Good to know. Thanks, Doc."

"When he wakes up, he'll be hungry. Try to limit his sugar intake and get something healthy into him. Strap him to a chair if you have to."

Hmm, that has potential. "I'll do my best, Doc."

The doctor left and Gunnar snuck a peek into Bryn's bedroom. Even in the dim light his skin was pale, but he was breathing softly and seemed at peace. Gunnar left the door open a crack in case Bryn called out then went to take a shower.

An hour later, Gunnar was in the kitchen putting the finishing touches to his homemade mac and cheese when Bryn appeared in the doorway. He had on black cotton pajama bottoms and a ratty T-shirt. His feet were bare and his hair tousled from sleep.

"Hey."

"Hey, yourself. I thought you'd be out a while yet. The doc told me he gave you the good stuff."

"You have such pretty hair."

"And...I can see the meds haven't worn off yet." Gunnar put his dish of noodles in the stove. "Dinner is prepped. Just needs thirty minutes or so to finish off."

"Homemade mac and cheese? I think I love you." Bryn ambled over and rested his forehead on Gunnar's shoulder.

"Oh, you really are out of it, aren't you? How about we get you onto the couch?"

"Can we snuggle?"

"With you in this condition, the only snuggling going on will be between you and a blanket." Gunnar walked Bryn to the couch. He got him settled under a thick, woolen throw. "Nap if you want to. I'll wake you when the food is ready."

Bryn's eyelids were already drooping. "'Kay. You have such pretty hair."

Gunnar shook his head, smiling, then returned to the safety of the kitchen. He messed around tidying up, doing things he didn't really need to do until it was time to put the garlic bread in to warm. He tossed a side salad in some dressing then took it through to the dining table. Bryn was fast asleep, blanket pulled up to his chin, one slim bare foot dangling over the edge of the couch. Every possessive, protective wolf instinct Gunnar possessed jumped into high gear. Bryn was young and beautiful but so vulnerable. Gunnar gripped the salad bowl a bit too hard. It hadn't taken Bryn long to get beneath his skin and the thought of him getting hurt was unacceptable.

"Keep it professional, Gunnar, Jesus."

"Talking to yourself, partner?" Bryn shoved the blanket down to his waist. "I was in bed. How did I get here?"

"Walked there on your own two feet. You were pretty out of it, though." Gunnar chuckled.

"The doc gave me some meds. My head hurt... When did we get back from the store? Where are my Twinkies?"

"You don't remember what happened?"

Bryn frowned. "You were at the checkout. I was looking at chips. I could see you were at the front of the line so I came to join you and... Oh fuck. I touched someone. Someone bad."

"Yeah, then you passed out in the car. Warden had medical personnel waiting. While they were dealing with you, he and I had a debrief on the rest of the day but he'll want to go through it again with you."

"Deep joy."

"You want to talk about it?"

"Nope. I want to gorge myself on mac and cheese. Seriously, Gunnar, it smells amazing."

"Wait 'til you've tasted it. You can have a Twinkie for dessert."

"You're teasing me. Did I say anything dumb while I was out of my head?"

"No, nothing. You passed out on the couch. I was surprised you could walk about at all."

"Sedatives don't work that well on me. Bit patchy."

"Good to know. Give me a couple minutes." Gunnar brought through the hot dishes. He'd barely put them on the table when Bryn took his seat and had a fork in his hand.

"What? I'm starving."

"So help yourself."

Gunnar was amazed how much food Bryn put away. "You have a wolf-sized appetite."

"Always do after" — Bryn wiggled his fingers — "you know, after I've done my thing. Especially more than once. Makes me ravenous. Also, this is the best mac and cheese I've ever tasted. The garlic bread is good too."

"You want more salad?"

Bryn wrinkled his nose. "Not so keen on the rabbit food but whatever you put on it made it taste good." He finally stopped eating after his third helping. "I guess I should do the dishes."

"You can help me load the dishwasher."

Bryn yawned. "Sounds like a good deal."

"Then it's back to bed for you."

"Yeah, sorry. I'll sleep all night then be back to normal in the morning."

"How about I give you a pass on the dishes this once. Go sleep. And the Twinkies are in the cupboard next to the one with the flatware." Gunnar watched him go and smiled at the rustling coming from the kitchen. The dishes could wait a while. Once Bryn had gone back to bed, Gunnar made himself a coffee then watched trash TV on the couch for a while. There was so much stuff rolling around in his head about his new job, about Bryn, about the day they'd been through, and what they might be expected to do in the future, shutting that down was a challenge. He massaged his neck. *Well nobody said this would be easy. Get a grip and go load the dishwasher or that mac and cheese will have set like concrete.*

Chapter Six

Gunnar stared at Warden across the conference room table. "You want us to fit an investigation based on not very much—no offense, Bryn—in between all this other stuff?" He gestured at the array of folders spread across the table.

Warden blinked. "Yes. You have a problem with that? You're a detective. Detect."

Bryn made a strange sound somewhere between snorting and choking.

Gunnar glared at him. "You have something to add, mister?"

"Nope."

"Wise decision."

Warden got to his feet. "Assess the case. I'll provide administrative support so you won't have to do the grunt work. It'll be good for Bryn to do something other than read people."

And there's the kill switch. Fuck. "Fine. Don't expect miracles."

"You've already got one of those working with you, Gunnar. This'll be a breeze." Warden went to the door. "You have my number if you need me. I'll be off-site for the rest of the day."

"Is there steam coming out of my ears?" Gunnar asked, staring at the now closed door.

"Your hair has come loose, I can't tell."

Gunnar growled and redid his messy bun. "That man is not good for my wellbeing."

"You're not going to go all feng shui on me and start rearranging the furniture, are you?"

"You're awfully calm about this shit-ton of work."

Bryn shrugged. "Don't have much choice, do I? No point in getting over-excited."

"I'm surprised you're not bouncing off the walls considering you had Twinkies for breakfast."

"I had some of that granola stuff you made, too, and besides, I need to rebuild my sugar capacity. I wasn't allowed junk food in training."

"Hmm, there's a reason for that. Where the heck do we start with this lot?" There was a tentative knock at the door. "What?" Gunnar yelled.

A bespectacled blond poked his head around the door. "Detective Ericson?"

"The big grumpy one," Bryn said.

"I'm, uh, Emmett. I'm your new admin." Emmett didn't venture into the room.

"You intending to work from the corridor, Emmett? Get your butt in here," Gunnar said in a softer voice.

"Yes, sir!" Emmett scurried in. He had on a diamond-patterned sweater-vest over a shirt and tie. Beige chinos and polished brown brogues completed the outfit.

"Don't call him that, he likes it a bit too much." Bryn smirked. Emmett paled.

Gunnar glared at Bryn. "How long have you been working here, Emmett?"

"Three months…Detective."

"Call me Gunnar. Well, that's three months longer than us so, I guess you know your way around the computer systems."

"Oh yes." Emmett put his laptop on the table. "Are we working here? Warden told me you have an office on the top floor."

"Yeah, I guess we should move. We'll probably get thrown out of here." Gunnar gathered all the folders then led a small procession to the apartment office.

Gunnar and Emmett took the two desks. Bryn dragged in a black furry beanbag.

"Where did that thing come from?" Gunnar asked. "It looks like some kind of dead animal."

"My room. It's comfortable." He positioned it against the wall then flopped onto it. "So where do we start?"

Gunnar shook his head. "Emmett, I want you to make a list. This will be a bit of a brain dump then afterward you can tell me how much of it you can manage, okay?"

"Okay." Emmett already had his fingers poised above his keyboard.

"Right then, we'll need any security camera footage from Walmart, all parts of the store and the parking lot. A list of all vehicles parked in the lot and their owners. Flags on any of those people with a record. Facial recognition from the camera footage once we have it and another list of people identified from that which will need to be cross-referenced with vehicle owners."

"You want camera footage from the surrounding area as well?" Emmett asked, tapping away.

"We'll need to narrow down the list before we attempt to track vehicles, but yes. Get the footage anyway. I don't want any of it getting wiped before we have our hands on it."

"On it."

"I want a list of unsolved murders from the Boston and surrounding areas. Lists of suspects, details of investigating precincts, FBI field offices."

"Might need Warden to get me some extra processing power," Emmett muttered. "You don't need to worry about that, though, I'll sort it out."

Gunnar was impressed. Emmett was clearly in his element. "Bryn, is there anything you can give us that will help narrow the search parameters?"

"White male."

Gunnar threw a pencil at him. "Seriously? Is that it?"

"It was a brief flash. I saw a man's hand, holding a knife. It was his left hand. There was blood on the knife, on his hand and sleeve. Traditional pale-blue, long-sleeved, cotton shirt, double button on the cuff. There were no scars or tattoos on the back of his hand."

"That's good. Very good. Were you seeing memory or the future?"

"Memory, I guess. I can't be one hundred percent sure but that's my default setting, if you like. I have to consciously switch to look for the future and I don't think I did that."

"What about this person's surroundings, could you make anything out?" Emmett asked. "Sorry!"

"Don't apologize. That would have been my next question and you're part of this team now, so don't hold back," Gunnar said.

Emmett's cheeks reddened. "Okay, thanks."

Bryn closed his eyes. "It's dark. There's some sort of plastic or rubber sheeting on the floor, splattered with blood, fresh and dried. Brick walls. Not much light, can't see the source, but it's flickering. It's cold. Not freezing, but chilly and…damp. There's a white marking on one wall." He opened his eyes. "I could sketch it. Also, I need coffee in the worst way."

"Good idea. How do you like your coffee, Emmett?"

"I can go make it," Emmett offered.

"No, you have work to do. Bryn can do it."

Bryn struggled to his feet, grumbling. "Strong and black for Gunnar, same for me but with three sugars, how about you, Emmett?"

"Cream, one sugar please."

Bryn ambled out of the room and Emmett glanced across at Gunnar. "I had no idea. I mean, Warden told me what he could do, but I can't imagine what it's like to live with that stuff in his head."

"He's learned to deal with it, but if he ever does anything that worries you, tell me. Part of my job is to make sure he's okay but I can't have eyes on him all the time."

"Noted. So, from what Bryn has told us I can put together a list of locations in Boston that might fit these parameters. Once I have his drawing of the symbol, I can look into that too. I'll get a map of the greater Boston area to go on the wall and sort out some pin boards and other stuff for this office. I don't see a printer in here so I'll get one of those too."

"I think you're going to be a great asset, Emmett. Remember to take breaks and feel free to help yourself to anything in the kitchen, okay?"

"This stuff is what I'm good at. I can also prioritize the other cases in all those files, look after your diaries, appointments, all that kind of stuff. I can produce background research, deal with other law enforcement agencies, book travel, hotels... Anything you need. I think I should also arrange for someone to come in here and clean the apartment, do laundry and maybe prepare some meals for the freezer."

"You can do that?"

"Warden said my job is to make your lives easier, to make time for you both to work. Organizing people makes me happy." He beamed and shoved his glasses up his nose.

"What are your working hours?" Gunnar asked.

"I'll work the hours you do and, before you say anything, that's in the job description. Think of me like a concierge in a high-end hotel. If you want it, I can get it. You wouldn't believe what kind of connections a network of law enforcement admins has across the city."

"I'm beginning to get a picture."

Bryn arrived with a tray of coffee, which he dished out. "I guess that until we get the footage we need, we should pick up another case." He returned to his beanbag.

"If you give me half an hour with the folders," Emmett said, "I can find something close by, or maybe where the cops or whoever can come here."

"Good idea," Gunnar agreed, "but how about we go through the folders together and you make notes because Bryn and I need to have a picture of the kind of stuff we have lined up."

"That would be great," Emmett said. "Give me a minute to set up a basic spreadsheet. I can fancy it up later." He took a giant swig of coffee then bent over his keyboard. Gunnar shook his head, not understanding Emmett's enthusiasm but relieved that he and Bryn had some help.

Emmett took the pile of folders, divided them into three then handed them out. "Who wants to go first?"

"Me." Bryn peered at the sheaf of papers in his first folder. "Potential miscarriage of justice, New York. Not too far away."

Emmett went next. "Interesting. Brothers both claiming the other killed their father. They are monozygotic twins so DNA evidence is useless. That's in Salem."

"This one is in Boston," Gunnar said. "Several suspects for an inside job on an armed robbery. It's an armored vehicle hold-up. Someone provided route details but there are several possible culprits."

The list grew as they took turns. It included juror validation, a kidnapping where a family member was suspected, possible false alibis, murder, rape, fraud... The cases stretched from coast to coast.

"Wow, this is depressing," Emmett declared. "So much misery."

"But all things we can resolve. Well, Bryn can."

"Hey, this is a team effort," Bryn protested. "No way could I do this on my own."

"I think we should go with the juror check. I can get them here because it's a Boston PD case," Emmett said. "The trial is about to start so they'll all be at the courthouse anyway. I should be able to get an adjournment and have them bussed here."

"How many are there?" Gunnar asked.

"Five. Will that be too many for you in one go, Bryn?" Emmett's brown furrowed.

"Not if it's a simple truth reading for each of them," Bryn said.

"Okay, well I'm going to need some time here getting everything set up," Emmett said. "It might be quicker if you guys went back to Walmart to view their security footage."

"In other words, you want us out from under your feet," Gunnar said.

"Oh, I wouldn't dream... I mean, that's not what—"

"Relax, Emmett. We'd be like spare parts sitting here. It's a good idea. We can take the bike over there. Can you call the manager so they're ready for us? I'd rather not have to explain what we're doing. Maybe say we're trying to identify a fugitive or something."

"Sure, leave it with me." Emmett beamed.

"If you can extract your ass from that beanbag, Bryn, how about we go do some work?"

Bryn held out a hand. Gunnar yanked him up.

"Does that not...the skin-to-skin contact?" Emmett said, wide-eyed.

"No secrets between us," Gunnar said.

"All he thinks about is chasing rabbits anyway, Emmett. Wolf stuff." Bryn affected innocence.

"The fuck I do."

Emmett didn't seem sure how to react.

"Don't worry, you'll get used to us." Gunnar gave him an encouraging smile. "You can set an example to Bryn on how to behave in a professional manner in the workplace."

Bryn pretended to wind his middle finger up and Emmett snorted with laughter. Gunnar sighed. "Might take a while, though."

Chapter Seven

Back at Walmart, Bryn and Gunnar locked up their leathers in the bike's panniers then strolled across the lot to the store.

"Did this ever happen to you before?" Gunnar asked. "Accidentally reading someone, I mean."

Bryn checked his gloves for the third time. "Yeah, all the time to start with when I was at the Facility. I can't switch it off, but of course they didn't know that at first. They wanted me to have more control, but nothing they did worked. People started avoiding me even more than they already had been. Because I always default to seeing memory — I guess it's the strongest signal or something — I saw a few things I shouldn't have."

"Like what?" Gunnar headed into the store and the inquiries desk.

"One guy had beaten the crap out of his wife. Two people had failed suicide attempts. Someone else had set fire to his neighbor's house. I could go on. Of course there was good stuff too, but it always felt like such an invasion of privacy. So much kinky sex, I can't tell you. Sadly most of them weren't gay, but you can't have everything."

"Wow, so someone decided you needed to wear gloves?"

"Yeah, my handler."

"I think you need to tell me about this guy...or woman."

"A guy. A vamp. Yeah, I don't talk about him unless I really have to."

"All the more reason to talk to me. Right, we're here." Gunnar spoke to the woman at the service desk while Bryn hung back. It felt good to be working on something that didn't involve him reading anyone. After a few minutes, the store manager emerged from a staff-only door and took them through to the security office, which bristled with monitors.

"I'm Drake Romano, the store manager. We had a call from Emmett at your office so we're all ready for you. Happy to help, in fact. I'm going to leave you with Dave, our security lead. He's already sent the digital files across to GCR but he's pinned down the rough time you guys were in the store so you can look at the footage here straight away."

"Sounds good. Appreciate the cooperation," Gunnar said as the three of them crowded into the tiny room.

"Dave can come find me if you need me for anything else," Romano said. "In the meantime, I need to go deal with a toddler in the hamburger freezer."

As they leaned over the monitors, Dave pointed out a pair of small legs sticking out of a freezer while the kid's mother attempted to extract him whilst juggling a baby in a stroller and a cart full of groceries.

"That happen much?" Gunnar asked.

"More often than you might think," Dave replied. He swiveled his chair around. "Dave Frederics. Security lead for this asylum. Nice to make your acquaintance."

"Gunnar Ericson and this is Bryn, my partner."

"Cops are getting younger and younger," Dave commented. "Or I'm getting older. Let me pull up the footage you want."

Bryn peered at the screen. It was weird watching himself and Gunnar as they traversed the aisles. Cameras had caught them three times before Gunnar wheeled the cart into the checkout line. After a few minutes, Bryn approached the back of the line and began to negotiate his way through.

"There!" There was the briefest glimpse of Bryn's hand brushing another hand.

"Who does that belong to?" Gunnar squinted and Dave stopped the playback.

"Can't tell. There are too many people."

"Play it on a bit, Dave."

"It has to be that guy," Bryn commented. He watched his own reactions. The moment he got the reading was plain.

"Black hooded top?"

"Yeah."

"He's aware of the camera position. He's keeping other people between him and the camera's line of sight. Hood up, and he keeps his head turned away when he gets to the checkout."

"Pays cash," Dave added.

"Definitely knows what he's doing," Gunnar said. "Can you make out what he's buying?"

"The belt's obscured. Wait, I see lemon juice," Bryn said as the man packed his purchases in a paper sack. "Honey, salt…sorry, I didn't catch anything else."

"Me either," Gunnar admitted. "I think we've got the right man, though. Most of the other people in the line are female. I can only see two other younger men, neither of whom is acting suspiciously, but we'll have to rule them out. Then there's the old guy with the walker. Don't think he's a likely candidate."

"The registers are digital. Give me a while and I can get the accounts team to search for the time of the transaction and get you a list of what he purchased."

"That would be great," Gunnar said.

"It may take a while but I'll get them on it right away."

"I guess we should get back to HQ then?" Bryn straightened. "We ought to get a treat for Emmett."

"You mean one for you with leftovers for Emmett, don't you?"

"How dare you? Casting aspersions on my kind gesture."

Dave was eying them. "Bakery has vanilla-glazed French crullers today, just saying."

"Let's go!" Bryn was already out of the door.

"Hold on a goddamn minute!" Gunnar turned back to Dave. "Do you have access to staff rosters? We'll need to talk to the cashier on that checkout."

I should have thought of that. Bryn hovered in the corridor. *Need to focus on the fucking job, not the novelty of being allowed out in public.* He scuffed the toe of his boot on the linoleum tile.

"Yeah, sure." Dave shuffled through some paperwork. "Here you go. That's Betty-Jo Jackson. She's off today. Next shift is tomorrow midday. Lemme

give you her details. She's only been with us a week."
He scribbled an address and cell number on a scrap of
paper.

"We'll try to catch her before she comes in. Thanks."
Gunnar backed out of the office.

"Sorry," Bryn muttered.

"What for?"

"Not thinking about obvious lines of inquiry."

"Hey, don't beat yourself up. You're new to all this
and the siren call of crullers is hard to resist."

"Fuck off."

"You want baked goods or not?"

Bryn lifted his glasses so Gunnar could see his eyes.
"Yes. I do." He pushed them back in place as the store
manager poked his head out of his office.

"You guys get what you need?"

"For now," Gunnar responded. "We might be back."

"Sure thing. You can find your way out, right?"

"Yeah."

"Hey, did you get the kid out of the freezer?" Bryn
called.

"Yeah. He was a little frosty but fine. Just another
day at the zoo."

Romano retreated into his office and Gunnar led the
way back to the store. Once Bryn had satisfied his need
for pastries they headed for the lot and back to the bike.

"You want to take the long route back?" Gunnar
asked as they both donned their leathers.

Bryn straddled the bike behind his partner. "Can't
believe I'm saying this but no. Let's get back. I want to
find out what Emmett has been doing while we've been
gone."

"Having a case of our own has got you excited,
hasn't it?" Gunnar revved the engine.

"Yeah. I like having something of ours to do. Helping out other people is fine, but you're a detective. It's fun watching you detect and I want to be part of it." Bryn wrapped his arms around Gunnar's waist and his pulse quickened. The throb of the powerful machine between his legs and Gunnar's proximity, along with the scent of leather, was a heady combination. *Why am I so attracted to him? This is so not the time for an internal monologue.* Bryn blanked his mind and focused on the bike's speed and the sense of freedom that came with it.

* * * *

Back in their office, Gunnar handed round coffee and crullers. Emmett inhaled his pastry then reached for another. "Love these!"

"Did you not take a break while we were gone?" Gunnar asked.

"Too much to do. I kinda forgot."

"Emmett, step away from the computer," Bryn said. "Or Gunnar will have to shoot you. I would, but they won't let me have a gun."

Emmett eyed him. "Why not?"

"In case I off myself." Bryn's tone was matter-of-fact as he reached for another pastry.

"Why would you want to do that? You're special. Unique. You're going to be able to do so much good." Emmett stood and stretched. His neck cracked.

"Wow. I wonder if they have a chiropractor on staff," Bryn said.

"I'll be fine. I'll do some yoga later." Emmett did a quick circuit of the room then resumed his seat. "I've set everything up on shared servers, so you'll both be able to see everything I'm doing. There's a spreadsheet listing all the cases from the folders and a brief summary along with a priority score. I've then ranked them by distance and grouped some together from the same departments and agencies. There's a link to the full file and I've started scanning everything in so it's more accessible. I've set up a separate area for your own cases—of course there's only one of those so far—and made tabs for all the relevant bits of the investigation cross-tabulated so it all links together. Easier to search. I…"

"Slow down, Emmett!" Gunnar grinned. "You've done more in a few hours than I could have managed in a month. Pace yourself."

"Oh, right. Yeah. My brain works fast, sorry."

"Don't be—this is all great but I'm just a wolf, not a genius."

"Yeah. What he said," Bryn chimed in. "I mean, I'm not a wolf. The not a genius bit."

"I've seen your files, remember. Neither of you is as dumb as you make out." Emmett rubbed his neck. "But admin is my thing. It's so satisfying getting everything organized."

"I think you're stranger than I am," Bryn muttered.

"Thanks for that contribution, Bryn. Did you get the security camera footage from the market, Emmett?"

"I did. I haven't viewed it, just loaded it into the folder."

"No problem. We saw it at Walmart." Gunnar handed over a slip of paper. "This is the name and address of a cashier we need to talk to. Could you track her down and set up an appointment for us?"

"Sure." Emmett took the note.

"And when we have time, I'll take you through the tape and point out some individuals we need to try facial rec on."

"Okay. Uh, Warden dropped by. He said you have to spend at least eighty percent of your time on requests for Bryn's help until the backlog is cleared. I took the liberty of arranging for those jurors I mentioned to come in later this afternoon. It's a mafia case and the prosecuting lawyers want to know if any of them have been threatened or bribed. There's a few more than I thought." He fiddled with his pen. "It'll be about nine truth reads, Bryn. I hope that's not too much. I know I said five earlier. It's not the full pool, but these are the ones that may have been within reach of the mafia boss's enforcers."

Bryn shrugged. "Stock up on Tylenol. It's doable."

"I wasn't sure...I don't want you to get hurt."

Bryn perched on the edge of Emmett's desk. "Don't worry about it. I'm not that fragile. Do we have time for lunch?"

"First people are due in an hour."

"Time for some of my patented chicken sandwiches," Gunnar said, cracking his knuckles as if he were preparing for a fight. "Watch and learn, boys. Watch and learn." He beckoned them to follow and marched to the kitchen. "Sit. Do not speak. Warm up your taste buds for a gastronomic orgasm."

"Sounds...interesting," Bryn muttered.

"Wolves like food. Lots of food. I can guarantee you've not tasted a chicken sandwich as good as this." Gunnar held up a finger to halt any questions. "Judgment by taste only." Bryn and Emmett exchanged a look, which Gunnar ignored.

"If I'd had more time to prepare, I'd have taken the chicken thighs out of the fridge to sit at room temperature for a while because they get crispier when you fry them, but life ain't perfect." Gunnar gathered the ingredients and equipment he needed. He whisked an egg in a bowl then in another stirred together panko crumbs, flour and salt. "Double dipping is the secret." He dunked pieces of chicken in the egg then coated them in the flour mixture.

"Double dipping sounds kinda fun," Emmett commented, drawing Bryn's gaze. "What?"

"Should I be worried about you?"

Emmett ducked his head. "Of course not."

"Riiight."

"Are you two concentrating? You need a good, deep skillet." Gunnar brandished a pan before splashing in some vegetable oil to heat. Sizzling sounds filled the kitchen as he laid the chicken pieces in the oil. "These take five minutes so while they're frying, we can prep the sides. Bryn, you can shred the cabbage and cilantro. Emmett, slice the brioche buns and spread them with yum yum sauce." He handed out the ingredients then supervised as his recently recruited kitchen assistants did as they were told. Once everything was ready to his satisfaction, Gunnar assembled four sandwiches. "Two for me. One each for you lightweights. Okay, eat." He pushed plates toward Bryn and Emmett, then waited for their reactions.

"I vote for Gunnar making lunch every day from now on," Emmett said around a mouthful of sandwich.

"Seconded." Bryn grinned. "This is fantastic."

"You're spoiling us," Emmett added.

"Ain't that the truth," Gunnar agreed. "The upside is I get to eat them too." He'd already finished one sandwich and started on the next. "Hungry wolves are unhappy wolves."

"You won't believe the amount he eats, Emmett," Bryn said.

"I have a friend who's a wolf," Emmett replied. "He once ate an entire lasagna, by himself. He still had dessert."

Gunnar grunted his approval. "Of course. Talking of, there's a pint of butter pecan in the freezer."

Bryn and Emmett both declined, citing full bellies, so Gunnar fetched the ice cream and a spoon. It wasn't long before he'd finished the whole tub.

"You done?" Bryn asked.

"That'll tide me through 'til dinner." Gunnar rubbed his flat belly. "You ready to go deal with these jurors?"

Bryn shrugged. "Whatever."

"Your enthusiasm is inspiring. Emmett, can you track down the cashier and arrange for us to see her as a priority?"

"Sure. I'll get right onto it. After I've cleaned up in here."

"You don't have to do that."

"I don't mind. You cooked after all, and you guys have to go work. It won't take long."

"Don't argue with the man, Gunnar." Bryn grabbed Gunnar's arm and towed him from the room. "I like washing pans even less than truth reading jurors."

Chapter Eight

The following morning, Gunnar went for a long run, showered then had breakfast alone. Emmett arrived and grabbed a coffee from the kitchen before heading for the office and Gunnar went to join him.

"Where's Bryn?" Emmett asked as he got settled.

"I'm letting him sleep. All those truth readings yesterday took it out of him. He doesn't complain but he was exhausted."

"Yeah, he didn't say much when you came back. He gets bad headaches, doesn't he?"

"What he can do is miraculous, but it comes at a cost. He'll be fine later. Grumpy but fine."

"How did it go? Oh, I have the report through. You must have been up late doing that."

"I hate paperwork. If I don't do it straight away it builds up."

"My ideal cop. So, of the pool of potential jurors, five had been tampered with. Two threatened and three paid off. Wow."

"Yeah. Not great."

"So what's the case?" Emmett hammered at his keyboard. "Oh, I see. Mafia money guy. He could bring down a lot of nasty people."

"Yes, Emmett, he could. A lot of powerful people who don't have much in the way of moral compasses."

"Suspected of working for Salvatore Russo, aka 'The Hammer'. He's never been convicted of a crime despite being suspected of racketeering, extortion, money laundering, illegal gambling, bribery, tax evasion, cargo theft and contract killing. Wow, what a charmer. Lots of financial stuff there, how did they bring in his accountant?"

"Some Dutch forensic auditor spotted obscure anomalies in the books of a company that looked legit but turned out to be a front for one of Russo's European operations. After that there was a domino effect. She's in a coma after a hit and run."

"A calculator can be a dangerous weapon. Poor woman."

"Yeah. So this case is important. Bryn has made sure it starts off on the right foot, though it'll be delayed now while action is taken to call new jurors."

"Is there any way that Russo will know who tossed a wrench in his gears?"

"In theory, no. In practice? His web is extensive. I came across the aftermath of his activities in my previous job more often than I would have liked. He's ruthless. Bryn's a target anyway because he's an augur, but he's bound to make enemies the more work he does."

"My sparkling personality makes me popular." Bryn slunk into the room, coffee in one hand, Pop-Tart in the other. "What time is it?"

"Time we started work," Gunnar said. "Emmett, did you reach the cashier from Walmart?"

"Yeah. She'll meet you at the Honey Dew's coffee place near the Walmart parking lot at eleven. Her shift starts at midday."

"Okay, what else do we have today?"

"An interesting one. Your FBI friend Agent Bell made a request. I've sent you the details already but, in short, he has a witness to a murder he'd like Bryn to read."

"Dubious witness?" Bryn munched his Pop-Tart. "Fuck, why is the filling in these things the temperature of molten lava?"

"Because you have to let the steam out, genius." Gunnar shook his head. "Carry on, Emmett."

"The witness is a nineteen-year-old kid. Address is a homeless hostel. He'd just finished…servicing…a client. The guy had left and the witness was saved because he was still on his knees and concealed by a dumpster. He's in shock and his mind seems to have blocked out what he saw. Cops found him behind the dumpster, rocking and crying."

"Christ on a stick, this world sucks," Bryn muttered.

"So why's the case with the feds and not Boston PD?" Gunnar asked.

"The murder has hallmarks of several other active cases. Once they got linked, Bell picked up the cases."

"Possible serial killer then?" Gunnar frowned.

"Yeah."

"Fuck's sake. How many serial killers are there in this fucking city?" Bryn drained his coffee.

"Difficult to estimate," Emmett said. "FBI intelligence suggests there could be anywhere from twenty-five to fifty active serial killers in the country at any given moment."

"Are you fucking with me?"

"No, Bryn, I am not. If you need some reassurance, advances in forensic science and technology, along with better investigative techniques, make it more challenging for serial killers to remain undetected for long."

"Oh, that make me feel so much better."

"Some aren't linked to multiple crimes until they've been operating a while and that could be the case here."

"Fabulous. Does Boston have more than its fair share of these psychos?"

"No way of knowing," Emmett said with a shrug. "The city does have two famous murderous alumni. You have to have heard of The Boston Strangler."

"I was only off the grid for three years, not an entire lifetime," Bryn responded.

"He was believed to be responsible for the murders of thirteen women, most of whom were strangled in their homes."

"In the sixties, right?"

"Yeah. Albert DeSalvo confessed to the murders, though there are theories that he might not have been the only killer. Then there was another one in the late seventies called The Giggler."

"I haven't heard of that one," Bryn admitted. "Why do they always get names?"

"He supposedly giggled while he was murdering young women, but it could be an urban legend. The case was never solved."

"Fabulous. So, what does Bell need?"

"Full read. He thinks this kid's mind is protecting him, but maybe you'll be able to see past it."

"Yeah. Won't be a problem."

"Set it up then, Emmett. This afternoon should work." Gunnar sat at his desk. "In the meantime, we can familiarize ourselves with what we know about Betty-Jo Jackson."

They worked quietly until it was time for Gunnar and Bryn to leave for their interview with Betty-Jo. Gunnar peered out of the window. Rain was lashing down and looked set in for the day.

"We'll take the car. It's miserable out there."

"Fine by me," Bryn said.

"We can grab lunch after we've seen her then go from there to see this witness. Will you let Agent Bell know our schedule, Emmett?"

"Sure…wait, there's a message coming in with a red flag."

"Red flag?"

"Means it's from Warden. Oh. Oh no."

"What is it?"

"Betty-Jo won't be making it to your appointment. She's been found dead near her apartment."

"Fuck." Gunnar went to look over Emmett's shoulder. "What else do you know?"

"Not much. Warden has people tracing anything and everything to do with your cases so someone must have picked it up. He'll clear it with the on-scene team for you to be there if you want to head straight over. I'll send you the location."

"This is because of us, isn't it?" Bryn said, pacing the small office.

"We don't know that." Gunnar wanted to make Bryn feel better but deep down he knew this couldn't be a coincidence.

"Yet." Bryn put on his gloves. "Let's go."

Gunnar had to fight down his frustration as he drove through heavy traffic made worse by the pounding rain. Bryn was silent in the passenger seat, his face turned away. Gunnar let him be. He had the mess of his own feelings to deal with and he was worried about what they were driving toward. Bryn hadn't been to a crime scene before and, though Gunnar already had an inkling that Bryn's training hadn't been a walk in the park, this would be different.

He slotted the Taurus between two black and whites, then grabbed his jacket from the back seat. Bryn already had on his coat. Black, of course.

"You ready for this?" Gunnar patted Bryn's thigh.

"No, but what the hell."

"Okay then." Gunnar got out of the car. Bryn joined him and together they walked through the downpour to an area cordoned off with crime scene tape. As they approached, Gunnar spotted a familiar face. "Special Agent Bell, we weren't expecting to see you here."

"Your boss called me, gave me a heads-up about the case. It's possible this is the same killer you're seeing the witness about this afternoon, so it may well become my case. Shall we see what the cop in charge has to say?"

"Yeah. We're looking for a Lieutenant Sullivan." Gunnar flashed his badge at the nearest cop, who pointed out the lieutenant. He lifted the tape so Bryn, Gunnar and Agent Bell could walk through. Sullivan was standing at the end of a narrow alley, peering into the gloom. Crime scene techs scurried around and a few yards away a tent had been erected over what Gunnar assumed must be the body.

"Sullivan?"

"That's me. Are you the guys from GCR? I got a call."

"That's us." Gunnar introduced himself and Bryn. "And this is Special Agent Bell, FBI."

"You taking the case, Bell?" Sullivan asked.

"That's what I'm here to work out. What can you tell us?"

"It's a real bad scene. We got a call this morning from a guy heading home from his night shift. He found the victim, a woman in her mid-thirties, who we now know to be Betty-Jo Jackson. This is only a block away from her residence. From what we can tell, she was attacked late last night, maybe on her way home. It's a quiet neighborhood, so something like this really shakes folks up. No obvious signs of a robbery, so it could be personal. We're still piecing it together, but this wasn't random. We've got people canvassing the area, and we'll be looking at any surveillance footage we can get our hands on." He pulled out a notebook. "I can tell you what the ME said, with a big caveat that this all has to be confirmed at autopsy."

"Go ahead."

"The victim has multiple stab wounds, concentrated primarily in the chest and abdominal areas, with some defensive wounds on the arms and hands, suggesting she tried to fend off the attack. The depth and angle of the wounds indicate the use of a sharp, single-edged weapon, likely a knife. Based on the wound patterns, it appears the assailant struck with considerable force. Blood loss was significant. Time of death is estimated to be around four to six hours prior to discovery, based on early signs of rigor mortis and lividity. That would put the attack between eleven and one."

"Anything unusual about the scene?" Bell asked. Gunnar gave him a curious glance.

"Well, yeah. I guess. There were rose petals scattered around the body."

"Fuck. Any sign of sexual assault?"

"Can't say. She was still clothed but until she's been fully examined…" Sullivan shrugged. "We'll find out soon enough."

A crime scene tech walked over to them. "We've finished processing the scene and we're about to move the body, so if anyone needs to see her in situ, now's your chance."

"Yeah, I should do that," Agent Bell said.

"I'll take a look too." Gunnar waited to see what Bryn wanted to do.

"I'm gonna wait here if that's okay with you guys." He didn't make eye contact.

"Of course it is," Gunnar said. "You need to stay where I can see you, though, no going outside the cordon, okay?" Bryn nodded. Water dripped from his nose and hair. "There's a doorway over there you can stand in." Gunnar watched while Bryn crossed the street to take shelter. "Sullivan, can you have a uniform keep an eye on him?"

"Why, who is he?"

"He's an augur."

Sullivan's eyes widened. "In that case, yes. He's real then? I heard talk at the precinct."

"Real as you or me."

"I'll go wait with him myself, I've already seen the body and I've no desire to see the poor woman again."

Content that Bryn would come to no harm under Sullivan's watchful eye, Gunnar joined Agent Bell and they walked up the alley to the tent. Gunnar steeled himself. It wasn't his first murder scene and he had seen more than his fair share of dead bodies, but it never got easier. He was kinda glad that was the case. The day he got immune to the horror of what people could do to each other was the day he needed to find a new job.

Under the temporary shelter, Betty-Jo Jackson lay spread-eagled on the asphalt. The front of her clothing was torn and soaked with blood but if any had pooled around her, the rain had washed it away before her body had been protected.

"There was no attempt to hide her," Gunnar commented.

"No. This guy is bold. Sure of himself."

"You think this is another serial killer?"

"It's unlikely that a copycat could have known about the rose petals. This is the fourth body left this way. The method of killing has varied. Strangulation, suffocation, drowning. In each of the other cases, we believe he kept his victims alive for a few days. He used a knife on them but that wasn't how he killed them. And the bodies were all left in places where they would be found, though not necessarily quickly. No attempt was made to conceal them in any of those cases. And like here, the petals were scattered around."

Gunnar sniffed the air then bent close to the body. "I smell… Lemons."

"How did you… Sorry, forgot you were a wolf. With all the other victims, we think he put lemon juice or salt on the cuts he made."

"Fucking sadist."

"Indeed. Have you seen enough?"

"More than enough." Gunnar ducked out of the tent and tilted his head so that the rain soaked his face. He breathed deeply. He could see Bryn huddled in the doorway, Lieutenant Sullivan leaning against the wall next to him. "The witness you want Bryn to read later. Is it the same killer?"

"Yeah. We think the kid may have witnessed the body dump. He's scared out of his mind. He ran away from an abusive family and he's been living on the streets giving twenty-dollar blow jobs to get by. He's on his knees in a filthy alley, just finished with a client, and hears a sound. He was scared it might be the cops so he hid. He didn't have a great view but he's so fucking scared that he can't remember whether he saw anything or not. Even if it's buried, it's likely to be his most powerful memory, so we're hoping Bryn will be able to see the details."

"Not surprised the kid's traumatized. Bryn says a memory block is no barrier to him."

"What he can do is astonishing," Bell said. "But I wouldn't want to be in his shoes."

"Me either. Let's go, we may as well head for your office right now."

"Okay, I'll see you there. Wait for me in the lobby if you get there first and I'll sort out passes."

After thanking Sullivan, Gunnar explained what was happening as he and Bryn walked back to the car.

"Warden is not going to be impressed if we get these leather seats wet," Gunnar muttered.

"They're heated. Turn the heaters on. I'm soaked through to my underwear...well, I would be if I was wearing any, and I'm cold."

Gunnar gave his partner a side-eye. Bryn was grinning and Gunnar had to hold back a sigh. *Fucking kid knows exactly what he does to me.* Gunnar was glad his rain jacket was long enough to hide his bulging crotch.

Great. Why does the lupine sex drive have to be so high? I should bend him over the hood in the rain. There was a low rumble in the back of his throat and he guessed it was audible because Bryn's grin got wider. *Maybe I should bite him a little, mark him… Fuck, Gunnar, keep your mind on the job. Now is not the fucking time…but soon. Yeah, soon.*

Chapter Nine

Bryn didn't think he'd ever met anyone who seemed as utterly terrified of life as Talbot Dunne. He was only two years younger than Bryn but it was apparent that Bryn's group home upbringing had been way better than growing up with Talbot's toxic parents. Agent Bell had him in a suite normally reserved for child victims. Talbot was sitting on a couch, knees drawn up, gripping a pink teddy. He was wide-eyed and staring into space. When Bryn and Gunnar came into the room, he scuttled even further into the corner of the couch.

"Hey, I'm Bryn." Bryn walked across the room and sat next to Talbot. "You don't have to worry about him." He indicated Gunnar. "I know he's big and scary-looking but he's a pussy cat. Actually, he's a wolf, so I guess that should be puppy dog."

"He's a wolf?"

"Yeah."

"My best friend at high school tested lupine. He always looked after me when we were kids."

"Wolves don't like bullies. They take care of their pack. I guess the instinct is there even before the gene kicks in."

"Agent Bell told me you're an augur, is that true?"

"It is. Bell is one of the good guys, you know that, right?"

Talbot nodded. "He's been nice to me even though I'm a...a..."

"A man getting by the best he can in difficult circumstances?" Bryn nudged shoulders with Talbot. "You have nothing to be ashamed of."

Talbot relaxed enough to lower his legs. He kept hold of the bear. "You must think I'm pathetic."

"I think you're incredibly brave. You got out of a crappy situation and you survived. No way could I have done that."

"I'm not even any good at it." Talbot sighed. "You didn't need to know that, did you?"

Bryn chuckled. "Everything takes practice, or so I hear. What would you rather be doing?"

"Anything! Garbage collector, sewer cleaner, grave digger...anything! Just because I'm gay doesn't mean I want any old dick in my mouth."

"I get that, but did you have an idea of a career or college, anything like that?"

"It's going to sound real boring but I love computers. I wanted to get into IT."

"You mean you want to tell tech-idiots like me to turn it off and on again?"

For a moment, Talbot seemed uncertain but then he broke into a smile. "Yeah. I think I'd be good at it."

"Rather you than me. For me, ram is a male sheep and gigabytes are what I take when someone hands me a Twinkie."

"I love Twinkies!" Talbot exclaimed.

"Which is why we are definitely going to be pals. So, how do you feel about me having a poke around in your head?" Bryn softened his words with a smile. "You won't feel a thing, I promise."

"You can read my mind?"

"No, not quite. I can't see what you're thinking. I can see your strongest memory and that's what we're banking on. Even though you think you can't remember what you saw, it'll be in your memory. Your brain is protecting you but I can see right past the block."

"I want to help. What do I need to do?"

Bryn took off his gloves. "I need skin-to-skin contact with you. It works best if I hold your wrist at the pulse point."

"Okay." Talbot held out a very thin arm.

"All you have to do is relax," Bryn said. "You can think about anything you like, it won't make any difference." He wrapped his hand around Talbot's wrist and concentrated. Talbot's memory was strong and clear. He was kneeling on cold concrete in a dimly lit alley. To one side of him was a yellow dumpster and there was a strong smell of rotting garbage in the air. To the other was a haphazard stack of empty pallets. Talbot didn't like the taste in his mouth. He spat on the ground then unwrapped a stick of gum. He was putting it into his mouth when he heard a noise and froze. Bryn could sense his fear as Talbot peeked around the dumpster, a fear that escalated at what he was seeing. A man, wearing a dark hoody and pants, had entered the alley from the other end and made his way to a point about halfway down. Talbot couldn't make out his face but the body the man had slung over his shoulder was obvious. Talbot made himself as small as possible and held his breath. He watched in horrified fascination as the man dumped the body alongside a wall then kicked some trash over it. He straightened, glanced around then pulled a fistful of petals from his pocket and scattered them around the corpse. Talbot whimpered and the man stared in his direction. He took a few steps toward him and Talbot's heart pounded. A fire-exit door on the other side of the pallet pile creaked open and someone came out, heaving two garbage bags. The hooded man turned and walked away. Talbot sobbed and that was the last Bryn saw.

"Wow, that was fucking scary," Bryn said.

"Did you see what I saw?" Talbot asked.

"Yeah. Gimme a minute while I talk to my partner so he can make some notes, okay?"

"Sure. Not going anywhere." Talbot hugged his bear.

Bryn took Gunnar outside the room to relate what he'd seen. "He was lucky he didn't end up dead too."

"No wonder he's blanked it out."

"I don't think the killer saw him."

"That's good. I don't like the idea of Talbot being back on the streets, though."

"Me either. You think we could talk to Warden about maybe giving him a job and a place to stay for a while?"

"I think that's an excellent idea. That work for you, Bell?"

"The kid will die if he has to go back out there. Anything we can do to help, we should do."

"I'm going to go make the call," Gunnar said. "We should take him back to HQ with us later. When I'm done, we need to talk about these cases on your books,

Bell. Pool what we know and see if we can't work out some next steps."

Agent Bell nodded. "I'll go sort out a room and pull the team together. Bryn, can you take care of Talbot for a while?"

"Sure. Point me at food and we'll go eat. I'm starving."

"How's your head?" Gunnar asked.

"Fine. There was no resistance so it didn't take much effort."

"Did you look at his future?"

"No. I hope we're going to change it, so I didn't want to."

"Fair enough. Let's get going. We have work to do."

Gunnar wouldn't allow Bryn to go outside without him so Bell took him and Talbot to the staff restaurant. He handed over a code for payment then left them to it.

"Looks like we have carte blanche to stuff our faces," Bryn said. "I hope you're hungry."

"I guess. I'm worried about what happens next, though. I can't identify the guy I saw so I'm not useful anymore. They're going to put me back on the street, aren't they?"

"Gunnar and I have a plan. But let's get food then I can tell you about it and see what you think."

Bryn loaded his tray with a steaming bowl of chicken soup, two dinner rolls, an enormous slice of peach pie with whipped cream and a bag of chips. In a concession to Gunnar's concern for healthy eating, he grabbed an orange juice.

Talbot hesitated but then followed Bryn's example, mirroring his choices, except he chose English breakfast tea as his drink. They grabbed silverware then headed for a corner table. A few people eyed Bryn's dark glasses and gloves. It was apparent they knew what he was because there were plenty of muttered conversations and glances.

"How do you put up with that?" Talbot waved vaguely at the room as he took his seat.

"They're curious." Bryn sat down. "It's unavoidable." He took off his glasses and laid them on the table. "Might as well give them something to stare at."

"Wow. Pretty!"

"Why, thank you. That's better than freak or weirdo."

"I'd never heard of an augur until Agent Bell told me about you. Are there any more like you?"

"Not that I know of." Bryn focused on his soup, which was excellent. He was mopping the dish with the end of a roll before Talbot said anything else.

"What's it like working with a wolf?"

"I don't think of him like that," Bryn said. "Until he does something wolfy."

"Like what?"

"He gets growly when he thinks I need protecting. He eats enough for two and his senses are much sharper than a human's. He gets up at the crack of dawn to run, can you believe that?"

Talbot shuddered. "That's horrifying."

"I know, right? But other than that, he puts up with me. He can cook too." Bryn told Talbot about how he and Gunnar shared an apartment at the Gene Control and Research HQ and a little bit of the kinds of cases they were working on. He told him about Emmett and his genius with all things admin. "Do you think it's the kind of place you might like to work?"

"It sounds amazing, but that's never going to happen. I'm a homeless rent boy, Bryn. Who'd want to give me a job? Without a postal address I can't even get hired to flip burgers. Not that I'm putting down anyone who does that. It's good, honest work."

"Me and Gunnar have a bit of sway with the boss at GCR. Right now, he's putting in a word for you with Warden — that's our boss — to see if he'll take you on as an entry-level geek. I mean IT guru." Bryn chomped his pie. "Fuck me, this is good."

Talbot stared at him. "You'd do that for me? You only just met me."

Bryn shrugged. "We all need a helping hand every now and again. Eat your pie."

They were finishing their food when Gunnar came to join them. He had a plate heaped with pasta and salad, enough for three normal appetites. Bryn and Talbot exchanged glances and Talbot broke into a smile.

"What's so amusing?" Gunnar tucked in.

"I'd been telling Talbot about your voracious appetite, partner. You came through with perfect timing. Also, you need to get the pie."

"You do." Talbot nodded. "So yummy."

"So what did the boss man say?" Bryn asked.

"If Talbot agrees, he can come back to HQ with us. He can start work with the geek squad right away. Warden says they're always looking for new talent."

Talbot gaped. "You mean it?"

"Yeah. He also said you can use one of the residential staff rooms for a while and you'll get a budget for clothes and toiletries. Computer and phone will be provided for you."

"I don't know what to say." Talbot looked like he might cry.

"How about you fetch Gunnar some pie?" Bryn suggested.

Talbot scampered over to the counter.

"Did Warden give you any trouble?" Bryn asked while Talbot was out of earshot.

"None. He thought it was a great idea. I think that man's heart may be a lot softer than appearances suggest."

"Emmett will be pleased to hear that." Bryn grinned. "You know he has a huge crush."

"I suspect our Emmett is more interested in a firm hand than a soft heart," Gunnar said. "I'd bet good money that Warden is a Dom."

"No one's going to take that bet. It's obvious. He could have it written on his forehead and it wouldn't be any clearer."

"Which might be why he has the urge to care for those that are more vulnerable than he is."

Talbot returned with a massive slice of pie and placed it in front of Gunnar. "The lady serving guessed you were a wolf."

Gunnar beamed and gave the server a wave. "That is a good woman right there."

"I'm so excited," Talbot said. "And kinda scared, but in a good way. You guys have work to do, right?"

"We do. Should have thought of that," Gunnar said as he demolished his pie. "Gimme a moment." He typed a message into his cell and a few seconds later got a response.

"Okay. Emmett is coming by to pick you up, Talbot. He'll take you back to HQ, get you settled in and sort out some supplies for you, okay?"

"Sure. You'll be back later, though, right?"

"Yeah, and we'll come find you, but you'll like Emmett. He'll look after you. If you go wait in the lobby, he'll come in."

"How will I recognize him?"

"He'll be wearing a checkered sweater-vest. Today's was blue and yellow, I believe. He has a collection." Gunnar chuckled. "Give him half an hour. Meanwhile, we need to get our butts upstairs to meet with Bell's team."

"You sure you don't want more pie?" Bryn asked. "We could get some to go. It's Bell's dime."

"I like the way you think." Gunnar went over to talk to the lady he'd waved to before.

"You okay with this?" Bryn asked Talbot. "Things are moving pretty fast."

"More than okay! I can't believe how amazing you guys are being. I won't let you down, I promise."

"In that case, we'll see you later. You should come join me and Gunnar for dinner. I want him to make sliders tonight and if the two of us gang up on him, he won't stand a chance."

"If you're sure you don't want some, you know, alone time?"

Bryn's face heated. "Oh, we're not a couple. Work partners is all." *For now, leastways.*

"Sorry! I thought... I don't know. You guys seem so in tune with each other. My bad."

"Don't worry about it. We've not known each other very long but I guess we do fit well. Warden chose Gunnar for me... Seems he knew what he was doing, much as I hate to admit it."

"Your boss sounds scary."

"Your boss too now." Bryn chuckled. "He's not so bad. I've had worse." *So much worse.*

Gunnar, box of pie in hand, was waiting. "Bell said he'd meet us outside the elevator one floor up."

Bryn put his glasses back on before trailing Gunnar to the elevator. Once they were inside, he decided to poke the bear — or wolf, in this case.

"Talbot thought we were a couple," he said, without preamble.

"Yeah? Cool." Gunnar didn't even flinch.

What the actual fuck? Bryn fidgeted. "You don't mind?"

"Nope."

"Oh." *That didn't create the response I was expecting.* "Why not?"

"You're the one who can see the future. Look a bit harder."

Bryn gaped. *What? Why? When?* His dick twitched. Gunnar's expression hadn't changed. He exuded absolute confidence as if he hadn't declared his intentions out loud and without consultation. Bryn's snark gene seemed to be taking a vacation because he had no idea what to say. The elevator door slid open and Agent Bell was waiting. Bryn had to switch his mind back to the case and he had no idea how he was going to get through the meeting.

"Hey, guys. All good?" Bell gestured at them to follow him. "I see you found the pie."

"Yeah. It's great pie and everything's good." Gunnar gave Bryn a knowing side-eye. "We're all sorted with Talbot, so score one for the good guys."

"I've got people setting up an operations room right now. We can meet in there."

The room Bell led them to was a hive of activity but he called people to order and everyone found somewhere to sit, albeit on tables and cabinets as there weren't enough chairs for everyone. Gunnar lounged against a wall while Bryn sat on a pile of equipment boxes.

"Everyone, meet Detective Gunnar Ericson of the GCR team and augur Bryn Ashton." Bryn shrank down as all eyes turned to him. "Yeah, yeah, count yourselves lucky we have access to their skills. Other agencies will be invading this place to get to them, so I want you keeping your mouths shut about their involvement, got it?"

There was a murmur of agreement.

"Okay, we are now certain that we have a serial killer operating in the Boston area. We'll be following the usual protocols for dealing with the case. For those of you who are new to this, or in need of a reminder, our taking over the case has been agreed with both local and state law enforcement. This team will be the basis of our task force."

"Are we getting behavioral analysis support, boss?" one of the other agents piped up.

"Yes. The BAU will be putting together a profile based on the crime scene evidence and patterns. *We* will be studying the victims to understand why they were targeted. We'll be bringing in all the information from the crime scene investigations that have already taken place." Bell scanned the room. "Agent Chang will be leading on data management and analysis and squeezing anything interesting out of VICAP. That's the Violent Criminal Apprehension Program, for those who may not be familiar."

Chang raised his hand in acknowledgment. "I want tight control on public and media engagement. We need to manage the flow of information. I don't want this sensationalized or causing public panic, so no discussing the case outside of this room."

Bryn glanced around at the group. He saw serious faces — committed, determined people.

"Before we get into it, I want to summarize the four known cases we have so far. You want to talk about the first one chronologically, Hernandez?"

A female agent in a dark blue pants suit, her hair in an immaculate bun, went to the front of the room. "We believe victim one to be Eleanor Evans, known as Ellie, aged thirty-two. A homemaker with two preschoolers. No criminal record or dubious associates. Husband had a rock-solid alibi and was destroyed by his wife's death. We've worked out that she disappeared between one and three in the afternoon on her way to kindergarten to pick up the kids. She was found three days later on the side of Silver Hill Road in Concord covered in petals. She was pretty cut up, but autopsy found cause of death to be drowning. Any questions?"

"What kind of petals?"

Bryn didn't see who asked the question.

"Red rose," Hernandez responded.

"One of our confirmed links," Bell added. "Victim two. That's with you, Yoshida."

Bryn eyed the craggy-faced agent, who looked to be pushing fifty. His expression said he'd seen it all and that nothing would shock him.

"Hunter Carshaw, graduate student at Harvard studying applied mathematics. Wealthy family. Dad's firm builds super yachts out of Fort Lauderdale. He was found six months after Eleanor Evans. Cause of death was suffocation but he was also cut up premortem. Found in Oak Grove Cemetery in Fall River. That's where Lizzie Borden is buried. Might not be significant. Red rose petals were found around the corpse. This wasn't picked up as significant because roses had been left on several nearby graves, so it was noted that the petals may have blown there." He paused. "No attempt to conceal the body."

"Victim three was a Vietnamese male, Phan Minh Tuan, age twenty-two, who worked in a family restaurant," Bell said. "He was found in Parker Street Alley, near the intersection of Boylston and Tremont. It's a narrow passageway that runs through the block between the two streets. It's often overlooked by pedestrians but connects various buildings in the area. Our witness to the body dump, Talbot Dunne, had picked up a client at a club on Boylston and the guy took him to this alley for a private BJ.

"Tuan had been strangled but there were multiple non-lethal knife wounds to the lower torso and legs." Bell clenched a fist. "And now we have victim four, Betty-Jo Jackson. Boston PD has handed this case over because rose petals were found around the body. However, what's more interesting is that Betty-Jo was a cashier at Walmart where our augur got an unintentional read on someone with blood on their hands. Someone who purchased lemon juice, which Detective Ericson smelled on Betty-Jo's body. I don't believe in coincidences, people.

"So, we're going to work up everything we know about the four victims. Look for connections. Trace their movements. Talk to their friends, colleagues and families. I want detailed research on every body dump location." He paused. "Detective Ericson, you have anything to add?"

Gunnar straightened. "Yeah, we've already started to piece together footage from Walmart both in the store and in the parking lot and surrounding area. Bryn has confirmed that the perp we're looking for is a white male, stocky build, no more than five feet ten and we know he's familiar with the security camera positioning in that Walmart. I'll get everything sent over from our office."

"Good."

"He's not going to stop," Bryn said and the room went quiet. "He enjoys it. I most likely saw his strongest memory and there are a few details from that that can be included in the profile."

"Excellent. Bryn also did a read on Talbot Dunne's memory and the characteristics of the person he saw match the Walmart guy."

Gunnar raised his hand. "Whoever killed Betty-Jo must have thought she'd seen something that might lead us to him. I don't think she was a planned victim."

Bell nodded. "Okay. Get to work people." The noise resumed and Bell turned to Bryn and Gunnar. "I think you guys can leave now. We've got a lot of groundwork to do, but we'll stay in close contact."

"This feels real nasty," Gunnar said.

"Yeah. We need to stop him and fast." Bell shook Gunnar's hand, then Bryn's. "You or Talbot remember anything new, call me."

"Sure." Bryn surveyed the room and the four pictures now stuck to a board. "Let's hope we get him before he kills again."

Chapter Ten

The following morning, Bryn went to find Talbot in the IT suite because he wanted to know how he was settling in. He poked his head around the door and was confronted by banks of equipment, rows of computers and a steady background hum.

"And this is why I don't come in here," he muttered. "I hate computers."

"Hush your mouth, young man." A large African American woman with a strong southern accent glared at him. "I'll have no blaspheming in this office."

"Yes, ma'am. Sorry, ma'am. I was looking for…"

"Hey, Bryn!" Talbot's head appeared from behind a monitor. "This is way better than I could have dreamed."

"You're okay, then?"

"I had the best night's sleep. I have my own room and bathroom! And Camille is my boss and she's setting me up on the systems and I'm going to get all kinds of training and…"

"Slow down!" Bryn laughed. "I just came by to see how you're doing. Gunnar and me are going to the courthouse for the day. I didn't want you to think we'd forgotten about you."

"I would never!"

"Have you finished interfering with my staff, Bryn Ashton? You may be an augur but you're not too big to put over my knee if you keep disrupting the smooth operation of my department." Camille had her hands on her ample hips and Bryn took that as a sign to retreat. He backed out of the room. "Good luck, Talbot." *You're gonna need it.* "Catch you later." *Jesus, are her eyes bulging? And why do people keep threatening to spank me?* He made a run for it before Camille made good on her threat, and went to find Gunnar.

"Are we leaving?" Bryn asked when he found Gunnar hovering near the exit. "I went to see Talbot. His boss is way too scary."

"Yeah, we need to get going, and Camille is a sweet lady. She'll look after him like he's her own son. Also, she makes the best callaloo soup. You in the right head space for witness checking?"

Bryn shrugged. "Sure. I'd rather be working on the Walmart serial killer case, but it is what it is. This mafia trial is a big deal too."

"True and it has already been delayed thanks to the jury tampering you uncovered."

"We uncovered."

"Agent Bell and his team have plenty to get on with on the Walmart case. Maybe they'll solve it without us."

"I admire your optimism."

Gunnar drove one of the GCR's armored vehicles to the courthouse because this trip wasn't just him and

Bryn. Warden was accompanying them and he'd given Emmett permission to join them, to gain some experience. Bryn and Emmett were in the back, Warden had claimed shotgun.

"Does everyone understand the process we're going through today?" Warden asked. "I know Gunnar does, but what about you two?" He turned, pinning first Bryn then Emmett with an intimidating stare.

"In theory, yeah," Bryn said. "But I've never been in a real courtroom."

"Nnnn…no, sir," Emmett stuttered, blushing to the roots of his hair.

Bryn stared at him then gave him a slow, knowing smile. Emmett's eyes widened and his cheeks got even redder.

"Pre-trial prep has already happened. That's when both the prosecution and the defense compile a list of potential witnesses. They swap lists to allow for objections and preparations. Most of the witnesses have been subpoenaed to ensure their attendance in court."

"Most?" Bryn questioned.

"There are several types of witness where it generally doesn't happen. If a witness can be easily discredited or has a history of perjury, people who don't have the mental or physical capacity to testify, those who are protected by attorney–client privilege or doctor–patient confidentiality, that kind of thing."

"And if they're outside the jurisdiction," Gunnar added. "Sometimes it's not feasible to compel attendance, especially if people are abroad."

"Because this is a high-profile case," Warden continued, "measures may be taken to protect the identity of some witnesses. They might testify from behind screens."

"What about the press?" Emmett asked.

"The court might limit media access, but this case has huge public interest. I don't think that's going to happen."

"So when do I get involved?" Bryn asked.

"Once the witnesses have been sworn in. They have to swear to testify truthfully. You'll read them to check that's the case. Where it isn't, we'll get you to take a look for memory and intent."

"Will this happen before anyone else is allowed in?" Emmett asked.

"On this occasion, yes. Opposing counsels will be there, the judge and court staff, but not the defendant or the public."

"And will they have been told that this is going to happen and how it works?" Gunnar asked.

"Only once they've all arrived. We didn't want anyone absconding before Bryn reads them." Warden turned away. "This is a bit of a test run for us and a first for the court system. With augurs being so rare, only the highest profile cases will have the option of our assistance."

"There's no parking at John Adams, I'll go to Center Plaza on Somerset, it's only a short walk from there," Gunnar interjected. His local knowledge meant that they were walking along the street less than ten minutes later.

Bryn stared at the court building. "Impressive."

Emmett bounced. "As well as the Massachusetts Supreme Judicial Court and the Appeals Court, this place has the Social Law Library, the oldest law library in the country. It's amazing. I've been there lots of times."

"Geez, you get excited by the weirdest things," Bryn muttered.

"No yucking on his yum. We all have our fetishes," Gunnar said. Bryn knew he was grinning even though he was walking behind him and couldn't see his face.

"I think Emmett has more than most," he said under his breath.

When they got inside and through security, Bryn couldn't help but be impressed by the courtroom. There were high ceilings with decorative moldings, wood-paneled walls and huge windows, though they were covered by blinds for additional security. The judge's bench was on a platform at the front, with the witness stand to one side. The jury box was on the other side. Separate tables for the prosecution and defense faced the judge's bench and behind them were rows of chairs for the public and media, separated by a low barrier. He tugged at his shirt collar, wishing he'd worn a T-shirt like he usually did. "Where do you want me?"

"Sit at the prosecution's table," Warden said. "That way we can get each witness to come sit next to you, then move to the public seating once they've been cleared. When you're done, they'll be removed from the courtroom until they're called to give evidence."

"Okay." Bryn took his seat. "Who's asking the questions?"

"I am," Warden said. "The judge has agreed to that. He's happy to be read, too. He's an old friend and a good man. He doesn't want there to be any doubt that the proceedings are fair."

Emmett moved to a seat in the public area and Gunnar took up a position in front of a window where he had a good view of everything. He took his gun out of his shoulder holster and held it with deceptive casualness. Bryn had no doubt he was ready to use it should he need to. Gunnar caught his eye and winked at him.

Stop looking so fucking gorgeous. Damn he's distracting. Bryn drummed his fingers on the table, both nervous and impatient. He took off his gloves and sunglasses. *May as well be all-in from the start.* Warden stood behind him, not helping his nerves.

There was a palpable tension in the air as the gaggle of witnesses came in, accompanied by three armed court security officers. The witnesses went to sit in the jury box. A few seconds later the judge arrived. Tall with a beaked nose and steel-gray eyes, his gaze flickered across everyone in the room. He hesitated when he got to Bryn but gave him a brief nod before turning to the collected witnesses.

"I'm Judge Franks. I want to thank you all for being here today. You've been briefed on what's about to happen and we'll get through it as quickly as possible so that proceedings can begin." He took the seat next to Bryn then offered his hand. Bryn took it. The judge's palm was dry and warm, his grip gentle. Bryn pressed the fingers of his other hand against the judge's wrist.

Warden stepped up. "Judge Franks, is there any reason you know of why you should not preside over this trial?"

"No."

"Truth." Bryn was relieved.

"Have you ever had any dealings with the defendant or with Salvatore Russo?"

"No." The judge was icy calm.

"Truth."

"And finally, has anyone bribed or threatened you in order to influence the outcome of this case?"

"No."

"Truth." Bryn let go of the judge's hand.

With the example set, Bryn got through the first three witnesses without incident. The fourth, a tiny middle-aged woman of Asian descent, was obviously nervous as she took the seat next to Bryn.

"It's okay," he said. "It won't hurt. You won't know anything's happening." Her eyes darted around the room but she extended her hand for Bryn to take.

Warden asked the first question. "Ma'am, is there any reason you know of why you should not bear witness at this trial?"

"No."

"Lie." As soon as Bryn spoke, the woman tried to pull away. She yanked her hand hard then stood, tipping her chair over.

"They threatened my family, said they'd burn my children alive..."

In the jury box another witness stood. "Me too. They had pictures of my wife and children."

Two more people got to their feet but before they could speak, Bryn heard a muffled metallic click. He glanced at Gunnar, whose sharp ears had caught the sound too.

"Everybody down!" Gunnar yelled. Bryn threw himself to the floor then crawled under the table. He tried to see what was happening but there was chaos with witnesses and lawyers running everywhere. Warden had a gun in his hand. Emmett had disappeared, presumably on the floor between the chairs where he'd been sitting.

One of the court officers fired his weapon and there was a scream.

"Why's he firing at the witnesses?" Bryn's panicked brain took a few seconds to compute that it was the court officer who was the threat.

Bedlam followed. Shrieks filled the air, witnesses trying to hide or pushing toward the exits. The other court officers scrambled, hands fumbling for their own weapons, but their colleague kept firing. One of them was hit and fell to the floor next to Bryn. Part of the guy's head was missing. Bryn squeezed his eyes shut. "Fuck." He turned his head before opening them again.

Not everyone was running. Gunnar rolled from cover and fired at the rogue court officer. The bullet caught him in the hip and he dropped to one knee, cursing. He fired indiscriminately, forcing Gunnar to dive to the floor.

He's too exposed! Bryn didn't know what to do but before he could move, a shot from the opposite side of the room took the officer out. He fell and his weapon clattered to the floor.

Bryn scanned the room, heart pounding. Warden, his expression hard as stone, lowered his weapon. Bryn crawled out from beneath his table.

"Is everyone okay?" It was another of the court officers who spoke. He walked toward Bryn and Warden.

"Yes, I..." Bryn gasped as the man grabbed him around the neck, pressing the barrel of his gun into Bryn's ribs.

"Nobody move or this one dies." He walked backward in the direction of the exit, pulling Bryn with him. "The boss will love getting his hands on you. The trial's fucked, you'll earn me a nice bonus."

"Let him go," Gunnar said, aiming his gun at the man's head.

"Not a chance. You won't risk hitting this one."

A single shot rang out and Bryn's captor dropped like a stone. Bryn ran to Gunnar, searching the room to see who'd fired. Emmett, white-faced, dropped onto a chair, gun in hand.

"What the fuck?" Bryn exclaimed. "Emmett gets a gun but not me? So not fair."

"That's your take on this dumpster fire?" Gunnar asked.

"Yes." Bryn pouted.

"You want this one?" Emmett held his out but Warden extracted it from his grip. "Nicely done, Emmett. I'm proud of you."

"You are?" A smile spread across Emmett's face and his eyes brightened.

"Always." Warden patted his shoulder.

"You see that, don't you?" Bryn asked Gunnar. "Those two..."

"Yeah, I see it. You okay?"

"Yeah. Those guys aren't, though." He gestured at the dead bodies on the floor.

"One injured witness too. What a fucking mess."

"Will this stop the case going ahead?"

"I guess."

"No," Warden interjected. "You can read the rest of them, Bryn. The threat has passed. Let's not give Russo what he wanted."

Bryn shrugged. "You're the boss."

"Indeed. Gunnar, if you could get the bodies moved and make sure the injured witness is given medical attention. Then we can get on with this."

The judge came to stand next to Warden. "How could these men have gotten past security vetting?"

"They may have only been paid off recently. Russo has money to burn. It's more important than ever that this trial goes ahead. We need to show him he's not above the law."

"You should get the augur a bulletproof vest," the judge said.

"Hmm." Warden scowled.

"More like a Kevlar onesie," Gunnar said.

"I'm right here!" Bryn yelled. "Line up the damn witnesses so I can go drown my trauma in chocolate milkshakes and overdose on Twinkies."

Chapter Eleven

Bryn wrapped his arms around Gunnar's solid body and relaxed. Being on the bike meant freedom, if only for a short while. He was beginning to crave these interludes where it was just the two of them on the open road. The last two months had been crazy busy. Agent Bell and his FBI team had taken over the Walmart killer case and were working it as a presumed serial killer. The mafia accountant's trial had concluded and they were waiting on a verdict from the jury. He and Gunnar had been working long hours helping with as many cases as possible and Bryn was tired. He was also finding it harder and harder to ignore his growing feelings for his partner.

The helmet mic buzzed. "I said I'd brief you as we traveled. You awake back there?"

"Yeah. I'd have fallen off the bike if I wasn't, wouldn't I?"

"We need to work on a way of strapping you on so that can't happen." Gunnar sounded amused. "The amount of work we've cleared recently, I'm surprised you can stay conscious."

"I could use a day off. You think we could sneak out without Warden or Emmett noticing?"

"Not a hope."

"That's what I thought."

"I can ask, though. There's a Wolf Run coming up that I want to do. You could come watch."

"I've heard of those. Didn't know it was a real thing, though, thought it was made up."

"They're real. A Wolf Run is a race and a hunt combined. I'll tell you more about it when we're done today, but we need to talk about the case now."

"So where are we heading?"

"Essex County. A small town called Boxford."

"Never heard of it."

"Me either, until Emmett gave me the case briefing this morning while you were still snoring."

"I do not snore," Bryn protested.

"Must have been the wildebeest you keep under your bed then."

"Fuck off."

Gunnar chuckled. "Boxford is small, population about eight thousand. Close-knit community, lots of farming. Bordered by Boxford State Forest."

"Okay, so what's going on in Boxford? Doesn't sound like a center of crime."

"Yeah, the crime rate is extremely low, which makes this case unusual. A kid has gone missing and Boxford Police Department is treating it as abduction because the parents received a ransom demand for a million dollars."

"How old is the kid?"

"Seven. A boy called Edwin Jones. Parents are Edwin Senior and Rosalie. They run a plant nursery."

"So why has this one come to us?"

"Local PD suspects the parents might be involved and the kid is an asthmatic, he could be at risk."

"Any history?"

"No criminal record for either parent. One ticket for speeding. Finances are shaky."

"So why would they be targeted for an abduction if they can't pay a ransom?"

"Rosalie's estranged father is Frederic Salt of Salt's Farm Machinery. He's loaded."

Bryn shifted his position, deliberately relaxing his shoulders. "So what? Local cops think the parents want to hit daddy up for the million ransom but actually it's for them?"

"I guess so."

"So why do they need us?"

"They can't find the kid and they want to make sure he's safe before they make any accusations. They want you to read the parents."

Gunnar took a wide, sweeping bend and Bryn tightened his hold. "They aren't going to agree to that, surely?"

"Which is why we aren't going to tell them what you are."

"If we do that, they won't be able to use my evidence in court."

"They're aware of that. They think they can close the case anyway but want to find Edwin Junior first."

"So who are we supposed to be?"

"Specialist trackers who are going to head into the forest to help with the search. All you need to do is shake hands with them before we leave."

"I get the search thing with you being a wolf, but I don't fit the profile."

"You're my tech support."

"Figures. You know what I do doesn't work so well if I shake hands, it's better with a pulse point."

"I'm sure you can figure it out."

Gunnar built up some exhilarating speed as he navigated the winding roads of Essex County. He slowed as they approached Boxford, which proved to be quaint, with a number of colonial-era homes, their white clapboard façades and colorful shutters standing in stark contrast to the dark backdrop of the woods. They circled the town green then the steeple of the First Church of Boxford appeared above the treetops. Jones' Plant Place was on the outskirts of town. Once Gunnar had pulled into a graveled parking lot and they'd dismounted, Bryn took off his helmet and scanned the area. Row upon row of plants stretched out to one side of a cluster of buildings. In the distance he could see several greenhouses, sunlight glinting off the glass panes.

"Smells good," Gunnar said. "Earthy and fresh." He took a deep breath.

"That sniffer of yours working overtime, huh?"

"Yeah. Wolves like trees."

"You know that's wide open for a comment about… Never mind. Not the time." Bryn turned away from Gunnar's challenging gaze and scrambled out of his leathers.

"Wolves do like to mark their territory."

Bryn swiveled around to find Gunnar leering at him.

"Stop that! You're worse than I am."

Gunnar shrugged. "You started it."

Changing the subject seemed like a plan. "You think that's where the family lives?" Bryn nodded at a large modern house to the left of the business premises. There were people milling around outside and he could see some uniforms.

"Let's head over there and find Sergeant Kaminski. He's our contact. He's in charge of the search and knows he has to maintain our cover."

"I should take my gloves off. It's not cold enough for it not to seem strange I'm wearing them."

"Okay. I'll talk the talk and make nice with people. You be your usual emo self."

Bryn stuck his tongue out at his partner. "Rude."

"There's better things you could be doing with that tongue. We should talk about that." Gunnar strode in the direction of the house and Bryn, gaping, trailed after him.

If Edwin Junior's parents were faking, they were doing a damn good job. They were standing with the sergeant at the front of a crowd of people dressed in outdoor gear and preparing to leave. Two groups departed before Bryn and Gunnar reached them but others were still milling around discussing grid references and locations in the forest.

Gunnar introduced himself to Sergeant Kaminski. "Specialist search team reporting for duty." He nodded to Edwin Senior and Rosalie. "Sir, Ma'am."

"Welcome, and thanks so much for coming out here, I know you guys are in demand," Kaminski said.

Edwin Senior held out his hand. "The sergeant here has told us about you. We really appreciate your help."

Gunnar shook his hand then Bryn stepped forward. He did a double-handed shake that allowed him to grip Edwin's wrist as well as his palm.

"We're so sorry you're going through this." He followed suit with Rosalie. "This must be incredibly difficult for you, ma'am." He stepped back.

"Sergeant, perhaps you could bring us up to speed with the search," Gunnar said.

"Let me get this last group on the way. Mr. and Mrs. Jones, you should go wait by the phone."

Rosalie burst into tears and her husband escorted her into the house, an arm around her shaking shoulders.

"Convincing, aren't they?" Kaminski said.

"Yeah, how sure are you that they're behind the kid's disappearance?"

"Ninety-eight percent."

"So why the search parties if the kid's supposed to have been taken by his own parents?"

"The ransom call. The threat was that the child will be killed and left in the forest if the ransom isn't paid by six tomorrow morning. We have to assume that he's already in there somewhere. The forest is inaccessible. There are very few drivable tracks and wardens patrol the most frequented areas. It's possible the child was taken somewhere days before we were called in and with the parents here, he might be alone."

"Let's go somewhere private and Bryn can tell you what he saw."

Kaminski gave Bryn a curious look. "It's true then, you're an augur?"

Bryn nodded. "Lucky me."

The three of them made their way to a storage shed that had a table set up in front of it with drinks and snacks for the searchers. There was nobody within hearing distance.

"Okay," said Gunnar, "what did you see?"

"A bit of a disclaimer first, Sergeant. These were really fast reads compared to what I usually do. My default is to see a person's strongest memory. Seeing their intent, or the future if you like, takes longer so I couldn't do that. I'd need more contact time."

"Fair enough."

"So, Mr. Jones' strongest memory is his wife telling him their son is missing. His emotions were intense. Desperate worry was the overriding feeling. I can say with certainty that he had no knowledge of his son's disappearance prior to that moment."

Sergeant Kaminski frowned. "Unexpected, but go on."

"Mrs. Jones' most powerful memory is of driving her unconscious child into the forest then trekking through the trees. She was with a man, who carried the child. She was annoyed, struggling with the terrain and impatient."

"Fuck. Who would have put money on the mother?" The sergeant's expression darkened. "At least our instinct to start searching was right. We could have wasted so much time already."

"It's *her* father who has money, isn't it?" Gunnar asked. "Maybe daddy objected to her marriage or there's some other reason she thinks he owes her?"

"I couldn't tell how long ago they took the child into the forest," Bryn said. "We need to go find him."

"There are coyotes and black bears out there," Sergeant Kaminski said.

"Show me the maps," Gunnar said. "We can direct the search teams to potential spots then Bryn and I will go out ourselves. A wolf's nose might help. Bryn, is there anything you saw that could help pinpoint a location?"

Bryn closed his eyes. His recall of what he'd seen was always perfect, though most of the time he wished he could forget. "Trees. A lot of fucking trees. The path is very narrow, overgrown. It's sloping downward." He clenched a fist.

"Relax," Gunnar murmured. "The smallest thing could help."

"Bird box! Up a tree. Quite high. There's a number painted on it but I can't see it all. Three something." Bryn opened his eyes, swayed and made a grab for Gunnar's arm. "Sorry. Head rush."

"Let me go grab one of the park wardens," Kaminski said. "They might know about the boxes." He ran across the yard and returned with an older woman. "Alice can tell us," he said.

"Alice Cranbrook, volunteer warden. There are fifty bird boxes out there scattered across several thousand acres of forest. They're part of a program to encourage blue-headed vireos, which have been seen nesting in the area. It's uncommon in eastern Massachusetts and is a rare nesting species in Essex County."

"And the boxes are numbered?" Gunnar asked.

"Yes and I have a map showing their locations on my cell."

"We need the locations for the ones numbered between thirty and thirty-nine."

After a few minutes, Gunnar had marked the positions of the boxes on a map. "We can rule out thirty and thirty-seven because they're close to wide tracks. Thirty-four is near water. That still leaves seven locations."

"How about you and I take the most remote?" Bryn said. "Then you guys can radio the others out to the search teams."

"Deal." Kaminski got to work and Gunnar pored over the map.

"The bike will get us within about a half mile. Then we'll have to walk. Hey, Kaminski, is there any cell coverage out there?"

"No, you'll need to take a radio." Kaminski tossed one over. "Channel three. I have a guy on this end."

"Okay, let us know if anyone else gets lucky first."

Bryn scrambled back into his leathers. "You think we'll find him?"

"I think we're lucky you're here. We have a good chance thanks to you." Gunnar fired up the bike and Bryn clambered on behind him. "Hold tight."

Gunnar rode fast. The lack of roads into the forest meant that they had to take a circuitous route to get as close as possible to their search spot. Bryn held on and hoped they didn't crash. They arrived without incident but Bryn was a little shaky when he climbed off the powerful machine.

"You okay?" Gunnar asked.

"Sure," Bryn lied. He stashed his leathers in the pannier, replacing the suit with a rain jacket. There was a chill in the air and a misty drizzle swirled through the towering conifers.

"You rode well. You moved with me." Gunnar sniffed the air. "Heavy rain's coming. Let's go."

Gunnar took the lead into the trees, moving at a steady jog. Bryn followed, keeping pace. There was a semblance of a track but it was narrow and they had to go one behind the other. Undergrowth clawed at Bryn's pants and the ground was squelching underfoot. Every now and again, Gunnar would pause to examine a broken twig or scrape in the ground. "Two people definitely came this way. Most traces are gone so it was a few days ago."

"That's good."

They kept going. Bryn was fit but he had nothing like Gunnar's stamina. He hoped he wasn't slowing him down, though Gunnar gave no indication of impatience. After fifteen minutes of steady running, they found the bird box. Bryn bent over, hands on knees, taking deep breaths while Gunnar explored the area. There was no obvious path from that point onward but in one direction the trees were more spaced. In the other it would be much harder going.

"What do you think?" Gunnar asked.

"You're asking me?"

"What does your gut say?"

Bryn thought for a minute. "They have to have built a shelter of some kind, or knew about one that was already built. A birdwatching hide maybe, or a tramp's hideout. I'd say that would be well hidden, so…"

"Yeah, I agree. Wait here while I look for a path." Gunnar pushed through hip-high undergrowth then disappeared from view. Bryn heard him cursing as he searched. "Here!" Bryn followed his voice and found him in a small clearing. "There's another path over there. I think someone deliberately disguised it. There's so much loose foliage that it's hard to tell." Gunnar moved toward the trail, sniffing. "I can smell something that isn't forest." He loped off and Bryn followed as best he could. Gunnar was soon out of view but the path was clear enough. The sounds of shouting reached Bryn and he increased his speed. Through the trees a tent came into view, a camouflage net thrown over it. Gunnar was struggling with another man.

"Get the kid, Bryn!"

Bryn ran across to the tent then dropped to his knees to crawl inside. Behind discarded food wrappers and other waste, a small boy stared at him, eyes wide. He was filthy, and tear streaks channeled the dirt on his cheeks. A muddy sleeping bag covered his legs.

"Hey, kid," Bryn kept his voice low and calm. "I'm Bryn and you're Edwin, aren't you?"

The child nodded. "I'm cold, mister."

"I'll bet you are." Bryn stripped off his jacket and sweater. "Come here and we'll get you warm." Edwin scrambled over and Bryn soon had him wrapped up.

"I want my papa." Edwin wrapped thin arms around Bryn's chest. He stank of sweat, fear and worse.

"Which is why me and my partner are going to take you to him right now," Bryn said. He reversed out of the tent then stood, Edwin clinging to him like a baby monkey. "See, no need to be scared now." He pointed at Gunnar who had his opponent on the ground and was cuffing his hands behind his back. He flipped the man over and Bryn could see he was unconscious.

"He ran into my fist." Gunnar shrugged. "My bad." He dragged him against a tree so that he was sitting up.

"You carry cuffs?" Bryn asked.

"That's where your mind went? Excellent." Gunnar grinned. "Hey, Edwin, how ya doing?"

Edwin stretched out his arms, reaching for Gunnar. "Guess I've been rejected," Bryn said, handing him over. Edwin immediately buried his head against Gunnar's shoulder.

"It's okay, little man. You're safe now." Gunnar tossed Bryn the radio. "You want to pass on the news?"

"Sure." Bryn got on the radio and let the operator at the plant nursery know Edwin was safe. There was a lot of whooping and hollering in the background.

"Get them to meet me at the road. I'll walk out with Edwin if you can stay and keep an eye on this piece of shit." Gunnar toed the man's body.

"Sure." Bryn relayed the information.

"Let me put you down a minute, kid." Gunnar took off his jacket and handed it to Bryn. "You'll freeze standing around here." He picked Edwin up again. "See if you can find something to tie this idiot's ankles. We don't know how long he'll be out."

"Did you kill the bad man?" Edwin asked, his voice muffled.

"He's having a little sleep," Gunnar replied. "I won't let him near you ever again." He nodded to Bryn then loped into the trees.

Bryn tore ropes from the tent and hobbled the captive's knees and ankles. Then he found a sturdy branch. "Wake up, you fucker. I dare you." He hoped Gunnar wouldn't be too long but in the meantime, the warmth and smell of his jacket were enough.

Chapter Twelve

Several hours later, Gunnar stopped the bike at a food stand on the side of the road and bought loaded hotdogs for them both. They took the food and paper cups of coffee to a picnic table and ate in silence for a few minutes.

"This is good." Bryn munched his dog.

"You have a bit of ketchup..." Gunnar reached across. He brushed the speck of sauce away with the pad of his thumb. Bryn's lips were soft and pink...tempting.

Bryn stared at him. "Uh, thanks."

He has the thickest, darkest lashes I've ever seen on a man. Gunnar distracted himself with coffee. "That was a satisfying case, wasn't it?"

"Yeah. That poor kid. I wonder what'll happen to him."

"I guess he'll be looked after until his father is officially cleared then he'll be able to go home. His mom will be going to jail and so will her boyfriend."

"I hope they rot."

"Yeah, the trauma is going to be with that child for the rest of his life. The only positive is that his grandfather is taking an interest. With mom out of the picture, maybe bridges can be built."

"I hope so. So many kids are growing up in group homes. Family is important."

"Your group home was okay, though, wasn't it?" Gunnar asked.

"It was good. The housemother was brilliant and the place was happy even though we didn't get many luxuries. I can't complain. I didn't remember my parents so it was all I ever knew."

"So are you ready to talk about what happened after that? Tell me about the Facility."

"You really want to know?" Bryn frowned.

"What you went through affects everything you do, so yeah, I want to know. It'll give me context. I want to know you better."

"If you buy me another dog, I'll spill. And a bag of donuts. Please."

"Fine. I can always go for second helpings." Gunnar bought the food and was soon back at the table.

"I don't know where it is. The Facility, I mean," Bryn began. "They drugged me so I was unconscious on the journey. Warden was there when I arrived and I saw him occasionally—I think he was checking on my progress—but he wasn't there all the time."

"He must have had you on his radar to work for him from the start."

"Yeah, but I didn't know that at the time. If I had to guess, I'd say the Facility was probably in the desert somewhere. It was definitely underground. There were no windows and no natural daylight. Exercising was all done inside."

"Sounds like a prison."

"It was for me." Bryn fiddled with his coffee cup. "My movements were monitored and restricted. There were other people coming through the place all the time for training but only short term. They avoided me, so I assume they'd been told not to interact."

"Must have been lonely."

"There was so much confusing crap going through my head I didn't have much time to think about it. Never was much of a socializer."

"Color me shocked."

"Hey! I can people... When I have to. Okay, when someone makes me, but that's so not the point. Let's just say I had plenty of time with my own thoughts."

"Okay, so who is this vamp dude you mentioned?"

Bryn sighed. "His name is Giles Delancourt, a British import. He came from some aristocratic family who relocated to the States for diplomatic work when he was a kid. He had his eighteenth birthday here and tested sanguine while he was at some private school in Washington State. That was twenty-five years ago and, lucky me, he never went home."

"I gather you and he didn't hit it off," Gunnar said.

"You could say that. So, like a lot of vamps, Giles went into science. Psychology to be exact. I saw his résumé and he had a shitload of degrees, had research papers published in respected journals and he'd written a couple books... His main interest was modifying behavior. Getting his hands on me must have been a dream come true."

"But your training must have been regulated, right?"

Bryn gave a short laugh. "That would be no. He was given free rein to turn me into a usable tool and that meant finding out exactly what I could do, what my limitations might be, the physical and psychological impacts, the effects of various stimuli and environments on my abilities. Alongside his research, there was a physical fitness program, diet control and education to degree level in law enforcement and criminology. Not that I ever graduated. The Facility isn't an officially recognized educational establishment, so that's something else they took away from me. I was supposed to go to Harvard."

"Describe him. I want to get a picture of him in my head."

"Not quite as tall as you, so about six feet. Dark, almost black hair with a bit of premature silver, very dark-brown eyes so they looked black in the right conditions. Pale skin. In fact, picture a charismatic vampire in an old movie and you've got him. He wasn't at the mild end of the sanguine scale, let's say. He's the most vampire vamp I've ever heard of, right down to the pointy teeth."

"Are you saying he could turn into a bat? Could you intimidate him with holy water and a cross?"

"Sadly not. Nor was he allergic to garlic. He did have a very strong fondness for blood and I'm not just talking about taking his steaks rare."

"You mean he..." Gunnar made fang motions at Bryn's neck.

"No, he did not bite me in the neck, Gunnar." Bryn took off a glove then turned his arm over. "He did it here." There was a scattering of marks across the inside of Bryn's wrist.

"What the fuck!" Gunnar was full-on growling.

"Calm down, Wolfy. It was a trade-off. The occasional snack in exchange for books, DVDs or access to the news. It was consensual. He never forced me."

"It's still wrong. He was in a position of power."

"Maybe, but he could have made me do it and he didn't. He didn't need the blood but said it was satisfying in a way raw meat and blood bags would never be."

"How else was he more sanguine?"

"He could move much faster than a normal vamp—like a blur—and he could also merge with the background in a way that made him almost invisible." Bryn paused. "He handled all my augur training himself and he had a sadistic streak he didn't bother trying to hide."

Gunnar's growling got deeper. "One day I want to meet Mr. Delancourt."

"I'm sure you and he would be best buds."

"So when you say sadistic, what exactly do you mean?"

"He pushed everything further than it needed to be pushed. He wanted to know how many truth reads I could do before I blacked out from the pain. You'd think once would be enough to test that boundary, wouldn't you? But not for Giles. He tried it over and over again. I lost days to blinding headaches and blackouts. He decided he needed to understand if I could do the same things under different conditions so he experimented with heat, cold, being wet…that last one was fun. He kept hosing me down with cold water between reads. For ten fucking days."

"Was he trying to kill you?"

"Sometimes I thought so. He wanted to know if I could still work under the influence of drugs or booze.

He had to strap me down for those. Forced me to drink alcohol. Injected me with who knows what. None of it made any difference. I can do what I can do but he was convinced there must be something that would stop me. He tried pain, a shock collar, all kinds of illegal shit. Then there was pleasure...forced stimulation...and denial...thirty days in a chastity cage. All the time I had to touch people, see their memories, test their truthfulness."

"Fucking piece of shit."

"Do you know what doesn't work? Touching dead people. The recently deceased or long ago. I can't do anything with a corpse." Bryn's hands were shaking. He hid them beneath the table.

"I'm not even going to ask where he got the subjects from."

"Neither did I." Bryn gave a wry grin. "It's over. In the past. I was too stubborn for him to beat...and too fucking angry."

"Took guts."

"Or blind stupidity. One thing, though, I've always been interested in the idea that the gene mutation has happened before. That it reemerges every so often and that all the myths and legends about werewolves and vampires came from people trying to understand what was happening. Maybe not so many people were affected way back. I mean even now numbers are small. What if the Black Death was the same virus? Spanish flu? There are a ton of examples."

"Seems possible, doesn't it?"

"In Eastern Europe, vampires are often depicted as reanimated corpses that feed on the blood of the living to maintain their undead existence." Bryn shuddered. "They can be repelled by garlic, crosses, and holy water, and can be destroyed by a stake through the heart. Something that I would have liked to try on Miles." His grin was feral. Gunnar rolled his eyes. "In China, the jiangshi are reanimated corpses that absorb the life force of the living. They have stiff movements due to rigor mortis and are repelled by mirrors and the blood of a black dog. Bit random. Miles had no issue admiring his reflection but I never saw him pet a dog and the Facility had a few German shepherds on the security team."

"The Native Americans had wendigos," Gunnar contributed.

"Yes! And the Ashanti people have the asasabonsam and the Bantu have the impundulu. Even the Aztecs had the tlahuelpuchi, a vampire that could transform into different forms and sucked children's blood. There are loads of others from cultures all over the world, some dating back centuries. Too many examples for it not to have been a virus."

"And viruses evolve, it wouldn't have always had the same effect on people. What about lupines?"

"Well, in Medieval European folklore, werewolves are often cursed individuals who transform into wolves during a full moon. They are typically depicted as bloodthirsty and driven by primal instincts." Bryn eyed his partner. "Silver weapons are considered the most effective means of killing them."

"Hmm."

"But... In Norse mythology, warriors known as ulfhednar wore wolf pelts and could channel the spirit of the wolf, enhancing their strength and ferocity in battle."

"I like that better."

"Thought you would. Anyhow, I'm boring you. I could talk about this stuff for hours. Books were an escape and Giles didn't object to me doing some research if it kept me quiet."

"It's not boring at all. We can talk about it more tonight if you like, but we'd better head back. It's getting late and it's been a long day."

"Yeah. You know, I've never told anyone else any of this."

"I have a trustworthy face." Gunnar gave a lopsided grin. "And I won't be sharing with anyone."

"You think I'm crazy?" Bryn got up from his bench.

"I think you must be as traumatized as that kid from today, but crazy? Nope. You're belligerent, stubborn and snarky, qualities that helped you survive. I see you, Bryn Ashton."

"Guess I'm well and truly screwed then. Won't be able to get away with anything."

"You got that right. Now mount up. Let's get home."

Chapter Thirteen

"So tell me about this Wolf Run," Bryn said as he pulled on his hiking boots. "It must be something special for Warden to give us all a day off."

"It's great," Gunnar enthused. "There are three or four a year generally and they are competitive events. They're not exclusive to lupines but you'd have to be an elite athlete to keep up if you weren't. There can be anywhere from fifty to a hundred competitors depending on the date, so they are the biggest gatherings of wolves that happen."

"That's a lot of hairiness in one place."

"And that is a shameful generalization, Bryn Ashton."

"You're telling me there are hairless lupines? Seriously?"

"I know one or two guys who like to shave their heads."

"Ha, who knew?" Bryn grabbed his jacket. "So what's it all about? A while back you said it was a cross between a hunt and a race."

"That's right. The organizers pick some remote area and lay a scent trail. You remember how I could find Edwin Junior because there were smells that didn't fit with the surroundings? It's kind of the same thing. It's a cross country run but there's no laid out course other than the scent. The start and end points are always the same, so it's circular and somewhere along the route you have to collect a flag. If there are any human competitors, they get given a set of coordinates to follow a bit like orienteering. Spectators are restricted to the start-finish line."

"So what happens in the woods, stays in the woods?"

"Yeah, it can get a bit rough."

"So what do you get if you win?"

"Bragging rights."

Bryn gaped. "You mean you put yourself through this and there's no prize at the end of it?"

"That's right."

"You ever win?"

Gunnar shrugged. "Not yet. Came close a couple times, but some of these dudes practice every week and I don't have a schedule that allows for that. I like the taking part, the banter, being around a bunch of wolves. It's fun."

"And I get to go watch. Yay."

"Would you rather be working?"

Bryn thought about it for all of five seconds. "No. Any day off is better than none, even if it is pouring with rain out there. Emmett better be packing a lot of snacks."

"I did!" Emmett exclaimed as he joined them. He was bundled up in waterproof gear and a purple bobble hat. "I went to the market and got a whole bunch of stuff. Anything with an E number and it was game. The competitors get food at the end of the run so I didn't even have to get healthy stuff for Gunnar."

"You sound excited," Gunnar said.

"Sure am. It's amazing I get the chance to see this. Thanks for letting me tag along, Gunnar."

"I'm happy to have you with us, Emmett," Gunnar said, "but this trip didn't have much to do with me. It was Warden's idea that we made it a team outing and he wanted you along."

Emmett bounced. "Is Warden coming too?"

"He is, but he's meeting us there," Gunnar confirmed. "He had some other mysterious errands to do in the area first."

"Just you and me for the snacks then, Emmett," Bryn said, rubbing his hands together. "It might not be such a bad day out after all."

"Well, if you two don't get your asses in the car, we won't make the start at all, so get moving."

"I'm taking shotgun," Bryn said, following Gunnar out of the building. A GCR four-wheel drive was waiting for them. "So we're going to Harold Parker State Forest. What's there?"

They all got into the vehicle and Gunnar set off.

"I can tell you about it," Emmett piped up. "I did some research."

"Of course you did." Bryn twisted around to show Emmett he wasn't being mean. He smiled. "Because you're always the most prepared person on the team."

"I'm not really the spontaneous type," Emmett said, ducking his head. "I like to know what's happening and keep everything organized."

"Which is why we love you."

Emmett blushed. "We're heading about twenty miles north of the city. The park spans three thousand acres and is mostly forest. There are some hiking trails but it doesn't attract as many visitors as other nearby parks, so it's ideal for a Wolf Run."

"The idea of running as recreation is beyond me," Bryn said. "Especially in a cold, damp forest. If I have to get wet, I'd rather swim. Preferably in a nice warm pool."

"I did some orienteering at school," Emmett said. "I like maps and clues and you don't have to run all the time."

"Marginally better," Bryn admitted.

"We have to head to the main parking area because it's big enough to accommodate everyone and there are amenities there."

"Is there a coffee place?"

"No, but there are some good places in Andover, which is only five or ten minutes' drive away."

"Five if Gunnar's driving," Bryn muttered. He settled back in his seat.

For once, traffic was with them, which Bryn put down to no one else in their right minds being out in the appalling weather, and they arrived in good time. Gunnar slid the car into a space in the already busy lot.

"Wolves must really like the rain," Bryn said. He peered out of the window. "Oh. Oh wow. This day is improving rapidly."

"Why?" Emmett leaned over the seat to take a look too. "Ooh!"

"You two want to put your tongues back in your mouths?" Gunnar gave Bryn a hard stare.

"What? I've never seen so many hot men in one place before and half of them aren't wearing much. Do they not feel the cold?"

"Not so much. Wolves are hot blooded and they're wearing running gear, they're not naked." Gunnar stripped off his top, exposing a skintight tee in some kind of shiny material, then pushed his seat back so he could shimmy out of his sweatpants.

Bryn had to force his eyes away from Gunnar's crotch. "Is it warm in here? We're steaming up."

"One of us is," Gunnar said. "I suggest you both stay in the car until the start. I'm going to say hi to a few guys I know."

"You are *not* leaving us in here," Bryn protested. "I want to meet all the yummy...your friends. I want to meet your friends." He pushed his shades up his nose then pulled on his gloves.

"What happened to not wanting to be out in the miserable weather?"

"Fresh air is good for me. You said so. Several times. And Emmett doesn't get out of the office often enough."

"No, I don't!" Emmett agreed with enthusiasm. "This is a very...scenic spot."

"You do realize that most of these guys aren't gay, don't you?" Gunnar got out of the car then fetched his runners from the trunk.

Bryn zipped his jacket and went to join him. "You said most, so that means that some are, right?"

"By the balance of possibility, they must be," Emmett contributed as he joined them. "However, my gaydar has been on the fritz since I realized I like boys."

He shrugged. "It's okay to look at the straight ones too, though, right?"

"No. No looking. No touching." Warden's gruff voice came from behind Emmett, making Emmett yelp.

"Hey, Warden, you okay to keep an eye on these two? I'm heading over to registration," Gunnar said.

"Sure."

Gunnar jogged away and Bryn made eye contact with his boss. "I was about to say you're not the boss of me, but you kinda are, so..."

"So you and Emmett are going to behave yourselves."

"Yes, sir," Emmett squeaked.

"Bring the snacks, Emmett. If Warden is going to spoil my fun then I'll need junk food."

"Me too," Emmett agreed.

"One or the other of you needs to be on a leash," Warden muttered.

Emmett blushed and Bryn watched his reaction with interest. *I think Emmett has a kinky streak wider than the Charles River. He's probably wearing leather underwear under his khakis. And Warden definitely owns his own leash. It's a match made in gay heaven.*

"You think I don't know what's going on in your head, Bryn?" Warden narrowed his eyes.

"I thought I was the augur around here."

"Hmm. You're trouble, that's what you are. I don't need gene abilities to tell me that." He glanced across to the crowd of runners. "Let's go watch the start."

"I feel like my character has been maligned," Bryn said to no one in particular.

Gunnar ran across to them. A few strands of his hair had come loose from his bun and his eyes were bright. "I can't wait to get started, there's such a great atmosphere. There are some really competitive guys running today, it's going to be a tough race."

"Do you have the scent?" Warden asked.

"Yeah, it stinks. I think they used some kind of dead fish to lay the trail. So gross. Still, it should be easy to follow." He turned to Bryn. "How are you guys doing, not too cold?"

"We're good. How long will the race take?" Bryn asked.

"The course is about ten miles, so with any luck the leaders should be back within the hour. If we were on flat, easy ground it would be quicker, but this is rough terrain, lots of obstacles."

"You're still going to run five-minute miles out there?" Emmett said, sounding astonished.

"Wolves, remember." Gunnar gave him a toothy grin. "Gotta go. Don't wander off anywhere, Bryn."

"Do you see a coffee shop anywhere? Bakery? Where do you think I'd go?"

Gunnar chuckled. "I'll see you in a bit. Be good."

Chance to be anything but would be nice. Bryn admired Gunnar's ass as he jogged away. *He can wear those running shorts any time he likes, though.*

There didn't seem to be a tape or any marked start line. The runners gathered in a crowd, whooping and yelling. There were even some howls. A klaxon sounded and the race started. Bryn was amazed at how rough it was. There were apparently no rules about contact and several competitors were sent tumbling to the ground. Within a minute they had all disappeared into the trees.

"So what do we do now?" Bryn asked. "Stand here like lemons freezing our asses off for an hour?"

Emmett handed him the snack bag and he cheered up. Delving inside, he pulled out a sack of Cheetos. "I love these." He tore open the packet and was soon stuffing his face with cheesy goodness.

"That's horrible to watch," Warden said. "But to answer your question, we can head into Andover and get coffee if you want to, or go for a walk. There are some ponds known for wildlife not far from here. We could be there and back in forty minutes."

"I vote for coffee," Bryn said.

"I wouldn't mind a walk," said Emmett. "Sorry, Bryn. You can have all the snacks."

Emmett's expression was so full of appeal that Bryn couldn't say no. "Fine, I guess. Gimme the bag." He let Emmett and Warden walk ahead of him, giving them a bit of space. Warden seemed to know where he was going and unlike the Wolf Run, this trail was well marked. *Could be worse, and now Emmett gets to talk to his crush. I need so many gold stars on my chart for this sacrifice.*

As it turned out, the ponds Warden took them to were picturesque and Bryn found he enjoyed wandering around. He snapped a few pictures with his cell to show Gunnar. *He'd like it here. Maybe we could come back on the bike one day. Fuck, am I turning into an outdoorsy type?*

"Time to go," Warden shouted from across the water. "If you want to be back to see the first finishers."

Bryn stuffed the end of a candy bar in his mouth then caught up with Warden and Emmett. Emmett's cheeks were rosy and he didn't meet Bryn's curious gaze. *Hmm, I'll have to interrogate him later.* As if Warden could read his mind, he gave Bryn a warning glare. Bryn affected innocence though he didn't think for a minute that Warden would fall for it.

The walk back didn't take long and when they got there, friends, family and onlookers were gathered at the finish line. The excited murmuring grew louder as the first runner was spotted and cheering erupted as he crossed the finish. Gunnar came in fourth, well ahead of the bulk of the field, beaming from ear to ear. Bryn waved to attract his attention.

"Hey, Gunnar!"

He trotted over. "That was so cool!" He was sweaty, his hair loose and his arms and legs were covered in scratches.

"You came in fourth!" Emmett exclaimed.

"Yeah? I lost track but I was hoping for top ten. I'll grab a water and an energy bar and say goodbye to a few folks. Would one of you mind getting my sweats and fleece from the car?"

"I'll go," Emmett volunteered. He trotted off.

"He's good for the team," Bryn commented. "He's not jaded or fake. I hope we don't ruin him."

"Upset him and you'll have me to deal with," Warden said. From his tone he could have been reciting a grocery list, not making a veiled threat.

"You say that about me, boss?" Bryn had no problem treading on dangerous ground.

"No." Warden didn't take the bait.

Emmett came running back clutching Gunnar's clothes. "I got them but there's something else!"

"Slow down, Emmett. Take a breath." Warden gripped his shoulder.

"Sorry, sir." Emmett gulped in a few lungfuls of air. "There's something under the wiper blade on the car."

"What, a flyer or something?" Bryn asked.

"No, a plain white envelope. And it's addressed to you, Bryn. I didn't touch it."

"You did good," Warden said. "How about you go find Gunnar, give him his kit and ask him to come straight back to the car. Bryn and I will go take a look." Emmett ran toward the crowd of runners. "You expecting anything?"

"Warden, who would know I'm here? After three years locked up underground, I don't have a bunch of correspondents. Maybe someone in the crowd knew me or something, I don't know."

They walked over to the car and sure enough, under the wiper blade, there was a white envelope. Bryn's name was written in black ink on the front in neat copperplate handwriting.

"The ink hasn't run. It hasn't been there long," Bryn observed. He reached for it but Warden grasped his arm.

"No. I'll get an evidence bag from my car. This will need to be forensically examined before you open it."

"But…it's only a letter."

"Which could contain anthrax powder, for all you know. Not everyone thinks you're a valuable asset to law enforcement, Bryn." Warden fetched a bag then removed the envelope. He sealed it carefully. "I'll take this back with me. The GCR lab can handle it."

Gunnar and Emmett joined them. "What's going on?" Gunnar asked.

"I'm getting love letters from a mysterious admirer," Bryn said.

Warden caught Gunnar up. "We should get back to headquarters. Emmett, you can ride with me. You two, straight back and no detours. Once the letter is cleared for nefarious substances and checked for fingerprints and saliva, we'll consider it together."

"Yes, sir." Emmett and Warden headed to Warden's car.

"You're taking this seriously?" Bryn asked Gunnar.

"Of course," Gunnar responded. "If this turns out to be a request for help or something innocent, no problem, but I don't think that's likely, do you?"

Bryn frowned. "I guess not. When are we going to get one normal fucking day?"

"You really want me to answer that?"

"No." Bryn got into the passenger seat of the 4x4. He tugged on his seatbelt, cursing when it didn't cooperate. Gunnar got behind the wheel then leaned across him to deal with the belt. He smelled of spice and sweat.

"You have to be gentle with it."

"Maybe I don't want gentle."

"Well, isn't that open to interpretation?" Gunnar put the car in drive then pulled away.

"And if I want it to be?"

"Fine with me."

Bryn's dick twitched. A bedroom tussle with Gunnar might not solve all of his problems right now, but it sure would help.

Chapter Fourteen

Gunnar had an itch he couldn't scratch. He had a bad feeling about the mysterious letter left for Bryn at the Wolf Run and he was impatient to find out the contents. Science took time, though, so after taking a shower and changing into fresh clothes, he decided to contact Agent Bell and check on progress on the Walmart killer case. There was a notable tension in the office. Emmett was busy at his computer and Bryn was on his beanbag, laptop balanced on his thighs.

"What are you guys up to?" Gunnar asked as he settled as his desk.

"I'm setting up an algorithm to interrogate data in..."

"That's great, Emmett. You lost me at algorithm. What about you, Bryn?"

"Doing some research on 'The Hammer'. Salvatore Russo. Know your enemies, right?"

"That trial is due to conclude later this week," Emmett contributed. "Depending on how long the jury takes to reach a verdict."

"I don't rate the accountant's chances if he ends up in the pen," Gunnar said. "Russo won't let him live. Too many secrets he could give up in there and it won't be difficult for a guy like Russo to get to him, even in high security."

"And the accountant will know that," Bryn said. "Maybe he'll try for a last-minute deal and witness protection."

"We'll know soon enough. I'll call Bell. I'll go sit in the kitchen."

"Where you can make yourself a snack," Bryn said, grinning at Emmett.

"Hey. I exerted a lot of energy on the Wolf Run, I need to top up the fuel reserves—especially as we missed lunch."

"Oh, I ordered pizza," Emmett said. "It should be here in half an hour."

"If I haven't told you how much I appreciate you recently, Emmett, I apologize," Gunnar said. "A quick snack then pizza. Excellent."

"I got two full-size meat feasts for you, ham and mushroom for me and Florentine for Bryn. Coleslaw on the side and some sodas."

"How did you know our order?" Bryn asked.

"I get to see the company credit card statements. I called the pizza place and they knew your regular order."

"You'd make a great detective," Gunnar said.

"It's just desk work," Emmett said but he was blushing. He hid behind his monitor.

"I'll fetch the food when it arrives," Gunnar said as he wandered into the kitchen. He grabbed a bag of chips and an apple then called Agent Bell.

"Detective, I was expecting your call."

"You were?"

"You *are* calling about Dr. Templeton?"

"Uh, no." Gunnar's hand hovered over the chips. "Why would I be?"

"Oh fuck. You don't know. I guess the grapevine isn't as quick as I thought, and we have been keeping this on the down-low."

"Keeping what? I swear, Bell, if I have to come over there…"

"Templeton escaped, Gunnar. Yesterday."

"You… He… What the fuck?"

"Yeah, he was being transported to a hospital appointment. He slipped the cuffs at the hospital and disappeared when the doc stepped out to get something. There's a huge manhunt going on for him but the higher-ups made the decision to keep it quiet in the hope we'd track him down fast."

"You have to be fucking kidding me. The man has a higher IQ than your entire chain of command added together. How long did it take you to catch him the first time?"

"Years, and you're not wrong. I'm fuming but the decision was taken out of my hands. I wanted to get the media involved but the director wants to save face, I guess."

"Why was Templeton at the hospital in the first place and not all cozy in the isolation wing?"

"Scheduled check for a heart condition."

"I'd better go give Warden a heads-up. I'll call you back later because I wanted a catch-up on the Walmart case."

"Okay, we've made some progress on that. I'll message you if we bring Templeton in."

Gunnar was glad his dubious expression wasn't visible to Agent Bell. He ended the call, gave his chips a look of longing, then went to find Warden. He found him in his office, glaring at his computer screen and muttering about incompetent federal agents.

"You've heard, then?" Gunnar stood in front of Warden's desk.

"How did you find out?"

"Agent Bell. I called him about the Walmart case and he told me."

"Shut the door, Detective, then take a seat."

Gunnar's anxiety spiked. "What is it?

"The letter that was on the windshield this morning, I've seen the contents."

"Why do I get the feeling I'm not going to like this?"

"Because you're not. In the light of what we've just learned, it's apparent that the letter has to be from Everard Templeton."

"Fuck. What did it say?"

"The letter's still in the lab. They won't find anything, of course." Warden pushed his cell across the desk. "Here's a picture of it."

"Hello again, Mr. Ashton," Gunnar read, "or perhaps I can take the liberty of calling you Bryn since we had such an intimate experience. I found our meeting fascinating and anticipate the next with relish. I'll be in touch. Yours in all sincerity, ET." Gunnar handed the cell back. "Fuck."

"Indeed."

"Are we going to tell Bryn?"

"Do you think we should?"

"Yes. Absolutely. He needs to be even more aware of his surroundings and besides, he knows about the note and it *was* addressed to him. He'll want to see it."

"Agreed. The letter will need to go to the FBI along with the forensic report. You can take it over to Agent Bell later today and catch up on the Walmart case at the same time."

"Will do." There was a tap at the door.

"Come in," Warden snapped.

It was Talbot. "Uh, there's a pizza delivery for Detective Ericson out here."

"Thanks, Talbot, I'll be right there." Gunnar avoided making eye contact with Warden.

"Out."

"Yes, sir." Gunnar made his escape. Talbot was hovering in the corridor. "Hey, Talbot, you want to come join us?"

Talbot picked up the stack of pies and handed them over, along with a paper sack of sides and drinks. "That's nice of you, but not today. I'm due in a training session on the dark web and I don't want to miss it. There will be donuts." He scurried off and Gunnar carted the food to the top floor.

"Pizza's here!" he yelled from the kitchen, after giving the pies a wolf-sniff test. Bryn and Emmett crowded into the kitchen and they all sat down to eat. "I saw Talbot downstairs. He was excited about some training session he was going to. He seems to be settling in real well."

"That's great," Bryn said around a mouthful of pizza. "This is so good."

The others agreed and the pizzas were soon demolished. Emmett had left a slice of his and was moaning about being too full. Gunnar eyed it.

"Are you gonna eat that?" he asked.

"No, I'm stuffed. Help yourself."

Emmett watched wide-eyed as Gunnar scoffed down the last piece of pie. "He has a bottomless stomach, doesn't he?" he asked Bryn.

"Apparently. There's never any problem with leftovers, that's for sure."

"Hey, I used up a lot of energy this morning," Gunnar said defensively.

"And you did real good," Bryn replied. "But now, how about you tell us what's on your mind?"

"What do you mean?"

"I mean you're keeping something from us. It's obvious — to me, anyway."

"What's my tell?" Gunnar asked.

"You're not bossing either of us around. You're too quiet."

Gunnar sighed. "You're way too perceptive for your own good. But yeah, there is something. It's not good news, I'm afraid."

"Is it about the letter?"

"Yes. I saw Warden downstairs, and he'd already read it. But for context, there's something else I need to tell you both — Dr. Templeton escaped custody yesterday."

"Everard Templeton? The serial killer?" Emmett asked, his voice rising.

"That's the one," Gunnar replied. "He got away from corrections officers during a hospital visit. The feds haven't found him yet, and I don't hold out much hope that they will anytime soon."

"Not good," Bryn muttered.

"That's an understatement," Gunnar said.

Emmett frowned. "I don't understand. I mean, obviously, it's bad that he escaped, but what does that have to do with you two?"

"It was before you joined us," Bryn explained. "I'm the reason Templeton was convicted."

"Oh dear." Emmett fiddled nervously with the spotted bow tie he was wearing. "The letter was from him?" he asked Gunnar.

"Yeah, I'm afraid so." Gunnar pulled out his phone. "Warden took a picture and sent it to me. Take a look."

Bryn took the phone and scanned the image before passing it to Emmett. "He's quite the charmer, isn't he? I don't think I'll be accepting any invitations to afternoon tea with him."

"Probably for the best," Gunnar said dryly.

"So, what are you going to do?" Emmett asked.

Gunnar toyed with his empty soda can. "There's not much we *can* do other than stay extra vigilant. It's Templeton's play now."

"This isn't the kind of admirer I need," Bryn said, concern etched across his face. Emmett's anxiety was written all over his, too.

"Try not to worry, okay?" Gunnar said. "He's got the entire FBI after him. They'll catch him — sooner or later."

"Let's hope it's sooner." Emmett pushed back his chair and stood up. "I'm going to get back to work. I think we should put out a call to the Wolf Run organizers and anyone else we can reach for cell phone footage. There weren't any security cameras in the parking lot, but maybe someone caught something — like a car approaching, or even Templeton himself."

"Good thinking," Gunnar said. "Bryn and I are heading over to see Agent Bell."

"We are?" Bryn asked, raising an eyebrow.

"Yeah. I want to hear what they're doing to track this psycho down. Plus, we can catch up on the Walmart case — Bell said there's been some progress."

"Okay, cool. Let me put on a fresh sweater. I managed to drop spinach on this one."

"I'll meet you downstairs. We'll take the car instead of the bike — it's easier to talk."

"Sure."

Gunnar wasn't fooled by Bryn's apparent nonchalance. If Bryn needed a few minutes alone to process everything, Gunnar was fine with that. He headed to the ground floor and stuck his head into Warden's office.

"I told him," he said.

"How did he take it?" Warden asked.

"How do you think?"

"Pretending he wasn't affected, then disappearing to think it through?"

"Exactly. He's 'changing his sweater' because of an imaginary stain. Then we're heading to the FBI."

"We can't stop working because of this," Warden said, "but keep a very close eye on him, okay?"

"Always." Gunnar shut the door and waited for Bryn at the bottom of the stairs. He heard the thunder of Bryn's footsteps as he came down them.

"How is it you make enough noise for a herd of elephants?" Gunnar teased.

"Loud stairs. Not my fault," Bryn replied with a shrug.

"Let's go."

Once they were on their way, Gunnar let the silence linger for a bit before speaking. "You can talk to me, you know. How are you feeling about this?"

"I'm not sure how I *should* feel," Bryn admitted, fiddling with a loose thread on his jeans. "Attracting the attention of a prolific serial killer wasn't exactly on my to-do list today."

"Fair point. When you read him in the interview room, you were only asked about his strongest memory. You didn't look at his future intent. Or did you?"

"Maybe."

"You're making this hard, Bryn. What did you see?"

"Nothing good."

Gunnar's patience was wearing thin. He ran a hand through his hair. "Bryn…"

"All right! I saw a bloody knife, bare skin covered in cuts and…a pair of black leather gloves discarded on the floor. My gloves."

"His intent was to kill *you*?"

"Not sure about kill. Torture, definitely. You saw the way he looked at me, Gunnar. Pure hatred."

"And you kept that to yourself all this time? It's been weeks."

"He was locked away. If I'd read him again that future would have changed so what was the point of sharing?"

"Oh, I don't know…so you didn't have to carry the burden of that knowledge alone?" Gunnar hated that Bryn hadn't felt able to share.

"I'm used to it. I don't want to fill other people's heads with the horrors I see. I don't want that shit in *your* head. It's my safe place and it shouldn't be polluted."

Gunnar gripped the wheel harder. "Is that how you see yourself? Polluted?"

"Don't you?"

"Not even close. Fuck, Bryn, I don't know how you deal with all the shit you've been put through but to me you're special. Precious. And I don't mean because of what you can do."

"Then why don't you do something about it? We've been dancing around each other since the day we met. You must know I have feelings for you. Very unprofessional feelings. The things I want you to do to me..." Bryn's voice trailed off. "Fuck, I didn't mean to let that out."

"You touch me all the time. You have to know I have feelings for you too."

"So..."

"So what?"

"So why haven't you pinned me down and fucked me to with an inch of my life? I know you want to...amongst other things."

"Because we're partners. Because I'm older than you. Because we've been getting to know each other and it *has* only been a few months. Besides, Warden would detach my balls and make himself a desk ornament with them if I went near you."

"There's nothing in GCR's rules that says partners can't date. You are six years older than me, that's hardly a massive age gap, and it's been several months, for fuck's sake. Warden I can't do anything about, but he does want to keep me happy-ish, even if he doesn't show it. Removing important parts of your anatomy wouldn't help with that."

"We're here, so this conversation will have to wait. Don't get distracted." *And that goes for you too, Ericson. Ogling that pretty ass could get us both killed.*

When they got into the FBI building, it was Agent Gomez, Bell's partner, who provided their escort to the incident room.

"Haven't seen you for a while, Gomez," Gunnar commented.

"I've been off work. Got some nasty complications from a bout of food poisoning and it took a while to get over it. Something called hemolytic uremic syndrome, which can lead to kidney failure. Never going near prawns again."

Way too much information. Bryn ignored the stares as he walked into the room. One or two people gave friendly waves and those he nodded to, somewhat surprised. "Where's Bell?"

"With the boss. He'll be back soon."

"Any news on Templeton?" Gunnar asked.

"Nothing. He's a ghost. We think he must have had help because several cameras that should have caught him leaving the hospital were out of action that day. There was also a fatal fender bender nearby, which meant potential witnesses were all looking the other way. Literally. If he got into a vehicle, nobody saw it."

"The GCR sent over the letter that was left on my windshield at the Wolf Run?"

"Yeah. It's gone into evidence but forensic analysis didn't come up with anything useful."

"Yeah, I could have told you that without rummaging around in anyone's head," Bryn said. He wandered over to the board displaying the photographs of the Walmart killer's victims. "What about the case we *can* do something about? How's that going?"

Gunnar came and stood at his shoulder. "Let's go sit down and give them time to tell us, okay?"

"Okay, I'm just...Impatient to catch this guy."

"And I'm sure they are too, but the investigation has to be thorough and you know yourself that there were a huge number of angles to close down."

Agent Bell arrived carrying a cardboard tray of coffees. "How about we go sit down at the conference table?"

"Is one of those for me?" Bryn asked.

"Of course. Sweet black coffee for you, drinkable black coffees for the rest of us." Bell put the tray on the conference table on one side of the room.

"I knew there was a reason I like you best," Bryn said, grabbing his drink.

They sat around the table and Bell cleared his throat. "Okay, here's what we've got. So far it has been a lot of legwork, but we *are* narrowing things down. Firstly, Gomez, you want to cover the cashier line?"

"Sure. We managed to track down all but one of the people in the cashier's line. We checked out the women as well as the men to cover all bases. They've all been cleared and by that I mean every one of them has a solid alibi for one or more of the dates the victims were killed."

"And the one you couldn't find? I'm guessing it was the guy in the hoodie," Gunnar said.

"Yeah. He was the only one whose face didn't appear on camera in the checkout line, in the store or in the lot. He went into the parking lot but if he got into a vehicle it was parked in the one camera blind spot and left via that only exit that isn't covered by a camera."

"He knew his territory," Gunnar observed.

Bell took over. "He did. We examined hours and hours of footage. We traced every vehicle we could identify that was in the parking lot at the time you and Bryn were in the store. We found one guy with an outstanding warrant who has since been picked up, two with outstanding parking violations, and a woman without valid insurance, but nothing more useful."

"So it was a waste of time then," Bryn said. He took a long swig of coffee.

"You can't look at it like that," Gunnar said. "A lot of investigative work isn't glamorous. This is just being thorough, ruling out all options."

"Don't worry, Bryn, I'm getting to the good stuff. So having narrowed down the suspect to hoodie man, we switched our focus to trying to make a link between the victims. It took a lot of digging because there was nothing obvious. They are different ages, sexes, races. They have different backgrounds and live in different parts of the city. They don't even have similar facial characteristics. Different eye and hair colors. We've done the analysis both with and without Betty-Jo because it's likely that her death is related to your visit to the store."

"Are you going to give us some good news?" Bryn said. He hated that someone may have died because of them.

"I am. We found a link. Walmart, would you believe it? The killer not only buys his groceries there, it's where he finds his victims."

"But these people were from different parts of the city, weren't they? Why would they all be shopping at that store?"

"That's the thing, they weren't. We found that Ellie Evans had called in there before on her way to and from her kids' kindergarten. Hunter Carshaw had a part-time gig with a delivery firm and had been to that store frequently, and Phan Minh Tuan had a family member working in the warehouse who he'd been to meet on several occasions. So there's the connection."

"That's good work," Gunnar said.

"That's not all. Gomez, tell them about the locations, and this is real weird."

Gomez tapped his pen on the table. "We put some people on researching the body dumps and they discovered something interesting. Ellie Evans was left on Hanbury Street in Concord. In the early hours of 8 September 1888, Annie Chapman's body was found on Hanbury Street in Whitechapel, England. She was one of Jack the Ripper's victims.

"We already knew that Oak Grove Cemetery where Hunter Carshaw was found is where Lizzie Borden is buried. She's best known for being tried and acquitted for the brutal axe murders of her father and her stepmother in 1892. It's one of the most famous unsolved mysteries in American history."

"Lizzie Borden took an axe, and gave her father forty whacks. When she saw what she had done, she gave her mother forty-one," Bryn recited the rhyme, getting several worried looks.

"What? It's a nursery rhyme."

"Moving on. Phan Minh Tuan was found in Parker Street Alley in Boston and that's associated with the murder of Carol Stewart in 1989. Carol was shot by her husband, who initially claimed that a black man had carjacked their car and committed the crime. That led to a massive manhunt and significant racial tensions in the city. But Charles' brother confessed that Charles had orchestrated the murder to collect life-insurance money."

"So, the first three bodies were found in places that could be associated with historical murders," Gunnar said. "This guy is one sick puppy."

"And the fact that his methods are different each time he kills suggests to our profilers that he's experimenting. He's looking to other killers for inspiration. It's likely that he has an obsession with serial killers, or murderers in general." Gomez's grin was fierce. "We're getting closer."

"This is great," Gunnar said. "I'd be looking at the employees next."

Bell nodded. "And that's exactly what we're doing, but that's a large store and it has over four hundred employees. It's taking time and of course those are people who are currently employed—we also have to take into account those who have left, retired… It's a huge job, though, thanks to Bryn, we can focus on Caucasian males."

"How about the kill site?" Bryn asked. "Did you get anywhere with the symbol I saw and sketched for you?"

"Unfortunately, an arrow in a circle is pretty common," Bell said. "We've had to switch our efforts elsewhere for the moment."

"Maybe we could get Emmett to take a look at that, Gunnar," Bryn suggested. "He might be able to magic up one of his algorithms if we gave him a few parameters to refine it with."

"Good idea. You have any problem with that, Bell?"

"Not at all. Any help you can give us will be welcome."

"Then I guess we'll get back to HQ." Gunnar stood and extended his hand to Bell. "You hear anything about Templeton..."

"You guys will be first on my call list, believe me."

Bryn didn't offer a handshake. Even with his gloves on, he wasn't sure it would be welcome, even though Bell had shaken his hand before. He took a last look at the board, making sure the four faces of the Walmart killer's victims were firmly burned on his conscience.

He and Gunnar left the building and headed out to the parking lot. Gunnar kept his body between Bryn and the building.

"This is the FBI, I think their parking lot should be safe," Bryn said.

"I don't want you getting any extra holes in you. I'm being cautious."

"And there's a wonderful image."

Once they were in the car, Bryn said, "We were only calling him the Walmart killer because of that touch in the checkout line, but turns out we had the name right all along."

"Yeah, it seems so."

"They've gotten further than I expected them to, if I'm honest," Bryn said. He stared at passing cars out of the side window as they drove along. "Dr. Templeton has got clean away, though, hasn't he?"

"I wish there was something I could do or say to make that better," Gunnar said. "He'll be tracked down eventually."

"Let's hope so. I don't want to be constantly looking over my shoulder wondering if he's going to jump out from behind a bush or something."

Gunnar chuckled. "Somehow, I don't think that's likely. I do think he'll want to mess with your head.

He'll turn this into some kind of game. He's arrogant and he'll think that he's far more intelligent than we are."

"He might be right."

"Individually, maybe, but as a team, I don't think so."

They traveled in silence for a while. Bryn wanted to bring up their earlier conversation but didn't know quite how. Somehow it didn't feel right, in the midst of everything that was going on, to focus on whatever there was between him and Gunnar. *Maybe later, when we're alone. There's so much work to do but I won't let him hide behind those lame excuses he gave me. I may have to deal with the uncertainty of being stalked by a serial killer, but I don't have to put up with Gunnar avoiding what I know he wants. What we both want.*

Chapter Fifteen

When they got back to the Gene Control and Research headquarters, Gunnar briefed Emmett on the image they wanted him to take a look at. He was excited and wanted to start right away, but because it was getting late, Gunnar sent him home. "There will be time enough for that tomorrow. You need to get some rest so that you can employ that giant brain of yours effectively in the morning."

"Okay," Emmett said. "You have to promise to tell me about everything you learned from the FBI today. I emailed you and Bryn a list of everything I've done today, and I've added a few new case files to the folder of future work." Emmett slipped on his coat. "You guys have a good evening, okay?"

"We will," Gunnar replied, turning off the light in the office and going to find Bryn. He wasn't in his room, but Gunnar could hear the shower running. It was very tempting to spy on him. Gunnar had no problem imagining Bryn naked, with soapy water cascading over his pale skin, his hair made even darker by the water. He shivered and gave his crotch a thump. "Behave," he muttered.

He went to the kitchen to investigate the possibilities for dinner and found that Emmett had stocked the fridge. "Emmett, you are a complete treasure," Gunnar muttered, feeling guilty that Emmett had gone home to cater for himself while he and Bryn were so well supplied. "He works just as hard as we do." He pulled a large cottage pie from the fridge. The label told him that it had been supplied by a local delicatessen, a family-run small business known for its excellent reputation and high-quality food and takeout meals. Gunnar realized now that they also supplied meals to cook at home. He had a good sniff to check for any suspect scents before he put the pie into the stove to warm, then picked out some veggies to go with it. He had just finished preparing them when Bryn came into the kitchen, his hair still damp.

"Thanks to Emmett, we have cottage pie and veggies for dinner, followed by apple pie and ice cream. He had the fridge stocked. You think he has any protection out there? He's kinda vulnerable."

Bryn immediately went to take a look. "Oh, wow, have you seen what's in here? And knowing the way Warden looks at Emmett, there's probably a whole team watching him that he won't even be aware of."

"Yeah, you could be right. We'll be eating like kings. And much as I like to cook, after a long day it's great that there's something to slam in the stove."

Bryn came to stand next to him. "You want me to help with anything?"

"I'm about done. Just need to throw the veggies in a pan. Do you want anything to drink?"

"A pint of brandy would hit the spot but I'll settle for hot chocolate. Can we eat on the couch in front of a bad movie?"

"Considering we are a pair of grown-ass adults, we can do what the hell we like. Food will be another fifteen minutes or so. Why don't you go make yourself comfortable and I'll bring the drinks through in a bit."

Bryn ambled away, humming to himself, and Gunnar got busy with the hot chocolate. When he took it through to their seating area, Bryn was on the couch, his feet tucked up under a blanket.

"That looks cozy." Gunnar handed him a mug and Bryn blew on it before taking a sip.

"It is and this is really good." He raised his mug in a toast. "Why don't you get under here?" He held up a corner of the blanket. Gunnar didn't say anything, just went to join him.

"You haven't put anything on the TV."

"I thought we should talk first. There isn't just an elephant in this room, there's a massive hairy mammoth."

Gunnar snorted hot chocolate. He wiped his mouth with the back of his hand.

"Give a guy some warning, won't you?"

Bryn snickered. "Sorry."

"No, you're not. So, what do you want to talk about?"

"Me. You. Us? All the excuses you gave me earlier today for us not being together were a pile of bull crap."

"Do you ever get to a point with subtlety?" Gunnar asked.

"Nope. Dancing around a subject doesn't get me anywhere generally. Look, all I want to know is whether you agree that there's something between us.

A spark. When I touch you, your future intent swings from bike rides in the open countryside, to running as hard as you can, to bending me over the nearest flat surface."

Gunnar sighed. "Not sure all of those surfaces were flat, but I like the idea of all three of those."

"And if you had to choose?"

"Don't push your luck, brat. Yes, there's a spark, I'm not gonna deny it."

"But?"

"Look, I think we should get the Walmart case out of the way. Focus on work while we get to know each other better. We're collecting a lot of enemies and I don't want to lose my focus when I'm supposed to be protecting your very cute ass."

"But that's not a never?"

"No. My willpower isn't that good." Gunnar nudged Bryn's shoulder. "Denial. Anticipation. Think how good it'll be when I finally get my hands on you."

"Oh God." Bryn moaned. "Try to remember I'm a twenty-one-year-old healthy male, Gunnar."

"I'm twenty-seven, my dick isn't fossilized just yet."

"Bet it gets hard as rock, though." Bryn snorted with laughter.

"Christ, you need a spanking in the worst way. I'm going to dish up."

"The food or a paddling?"

"Fuck's sake." Gunnar ran for the kitchen. He stuck his head in the fridge and sucked in some chilled air. Then grabbed a bag of peas from the freezer compartment to press against his crotch. *Why the ever-loving heck am I doing this to myself?*

After he'd plated two dinners he stood in the doorway for a minute, watching. Bryn had chosen something on the TV and was smiling at whatever was on. *He's mine. Soon. If I was an actual wolf I'd be howling right now.* Gunnar chuckled then headed over to the couch.

* * * *

The following morning Gunnar was up early and he ran longer and harder than usual. His dreams had been full of Bryn. That he was sleeping in the next room was torture and Gunnar needed to run it out of his system. He was back, showered and dressed before Bryn emerged from his room.

"You want eggs?"

"No thanks." Bryn grabbed cereal and a banana. "Is there coffee?"

"Brewing."

"You were out early."

So he noticed. "Yeah, felt the urge to run. Wanted to get in a few miles." Bryn sat at the table. Gunnar joined him with his plate of eggs and wholewheat toast. "What are you staring at?"

"You," Bryn gave him a lazy smile, licking his spoon slowly.

Gunnar didn't know where to look. He was being teased, and he knew it. He was saved by Emmett's arrival. The apartment door opened, and then they could hear Emmett taking off his coat and walking through to the office.

"We're in here, Emmett," he called.

"Good morning!" Emmett came into the kitchen with a beaming smile on his face. The day's ensemble consisted of a bright yellow sweater vest over a white shirt, navy slacks, and a navy bow tie with yellow polka dots. He had traded his usual polished brogues for a pair of the cleanest sneakers Gunnar had ever seen.

"Good morning to you, too. You're in a good mood today."

"I love my job. I can't wait to get started on investigating the symbol you sketched, Bryn. Ooh, is that coffee?"

"Yes, could you get me some too? Gunnar's been neglecting me," Bryn replied.

"Of course." Emmett delivered three mugs to the table but didn't sit down. "I'm going to start working. Oh, but before I do, on the way in Warden caught me downstairs. He suggested that Talbot and I sublet your apartment, Gunnar, because the current tenant is leaving for a new job. Would you be okay with that? It's much closer than where I live at the moment, and I'd be sharing with one guy rather than four."

"Sounds like a great idea to me," Gunnar said. "I left responsibility for it with Warden, so I guess you can get the paperwork sorted with him. It'll be good to know there are people I like and trust living there. Let me know when you guys are moving, and I can help with some of the heavy lifting."

"Oh, that's okay. Warden said he'd arranged for movers for me, and Talbot doesn't have anything to move. I'm going to do a call-out for people to donate things that he'll need for his room."

"That's a great idea. I did leave a bunch of stuff there, so you won't need kitchen equipment, and there are plenty of spare linens and towels in the closet. If you have any problems with anything when you get there, let me know. The faucet in the bathroom can be a bit temperamental."

"This is going to be such a good day, I know it!" Emmett bounced off with his coffee.

"I guess we should follow his example," Gunnar said. "We need to pick the next request to deal with."

"Oh, goody." Bryn took a long swallow of coffee. "Let's make it one where we can get out of the city."

"Any particular reason?"

"A change of scenery would be nice. Maybe an overnight. You know the way it goes…small hotel, booking mix-up, only one bed…"

"Get to fucking work!"

"Yes, sir! Love it when you get all growly, I can imagine the vibration around my cock."

Gunnar debated banging his head on the table but settled on collecting the dishes. *There isn't enough coffee in the world to deal with this.* He stacked the dishwasher then went to join the others. Emmett didn't as much as glance up from his computer. Bryn, flopped in his beanbag with legs outstretched, was on his laptop.

"I found an interesting one that shouldn't take too long," Bryn said.

"Okay." Gunnar sat at his desk and fired up his computer. "What's the reference?"

Bryn supplied it and Gunnar scanned the documents Emmett had stored in the folder. "Massachusetts General Hospital, amnesia case?"

"Yeah, that's the one." Bryn levered himself out of his beanbag then came to stand at Gunnar's shoulder. "A young woman was involved in a hit and run. She was found unconscious on a side street in the West End. Some lowlife took advantage and grabbed her purse so she had no ID on her. She took a knock to the head and can't remember who she is. The local PD thought I might be able to help find out who she is."

"You can see past amnesia? Isn't that memory loss by definition?"

"Yeah, but the memories are still there, the person just can't access them. I can't get past permanent brain damage or degradation due to a disease like Alzheimer's, but that doesn't apply to this woman."

"No. The doctor's note says there was some brain swelling but that she should recover fully in time. There's no reason why she needs to stay in the hospital but they need to release her into the care of someone who knows her. She was wearing a wedding ring."

"But she doesn't match a missing person's record?"

"Apparently not, but if she's from out of state, searching those could take a while."

Emmett peered around his computer. "Over six hundred thousand people are reported missing in the US each year," he contributed.

"Thanks, Emmett. Okay. Let's take it." Gunnar stood. "Let them know we're on our way would you, Emmett?"

"Will do. I'll text a contact name and I'll let Warden know where you're going. Are you going to take your bike?"

"Yeah, it'll be quicker. We'll grab some lunch while we're out so remember to take a break, Emmett."

"I'm going to meet Talbot and discuss moving plans. I won't forget."

The routine for getting their kit on and heading out was well-polished and they were soon on the road. Gunnar leaned into the curves, enjoying Bryn's arms around him. "You wish there were more cases like this one, don't you?" The helmet mike made a slight echo.

"It feels like a good way of using what I can do."

"What if her strongest memory is of being hit by a car?"

"It could be, but there might be something in her future intent to help. It'll be better if she didn't see the vehicle and that happens more often than not in hit and runs."

"Let's hope so."

"I had a test once where the victim had been deliberately run down. He saw the vehicle coming. He was in a coma and didn't survive."

"Did you get the plate?"

"Yeah, but the cops already had it. It was one of Delancourt's experiments."

That killed the conversation and Gunnar concentrated on the road. He and Bryn were getting out of their gear in the parking lot when his cell buzzed. "That'll be Emmett with our contact." He checked the screen. "Hmm, Emmett says to call him."

"Strange." Bryn came to stand next to him and Gunnar placed the call.

"Emmett?"

"Oh hey, Gunnar. Is Bryn with you?"

"When am I not?" Bryn muttered.

"Hi, Bryn!"

"What's up? I'm putting you on speaker." Gunnar checked to make sure there was no one in earshot.

"The jury came back in the mafia accountant trial. Guilty on all charges."

"That's good...isn't it?" Gunnar was puzzled.

"Well, it is and it isn't. Warden wanted me to tell you that word on the street is that The Hammer said he would offer a reward to anyone who brings Bryn to him if the verdict didn't go his way."

"You have to be fucking kidding me." Gunnar immediately examined their surroundings.

"I don't think Warden kids about anything, Gunnar. Anyway, I'm texting you your contact at the hospital. You need to go to Psychiatrics and ask for Doctor Sonya Tolliver. If you let me know what happens, I can pass information on to the police department."

"Okay, thanks, Emmett, we'll see you later." Gunnar stowed his cell in his pocket.

Bryn's shoulders were slumped. "Sorry."

"What for?"

"Being me."

"Hey, every cop wants a partner that's the target of a serial killer *and* a mob boss. It makes for an exciting life."

"Don't joke. What if you end up in the firing line?"

"In law enforcement, that happens every day, Bryn. Let's go do what we're paid to."

"But…"

"No buts."

Bryn stripped off a glove then grabbed Gunnar's hand. He squeezed his eyes shut. "Oh!" He blushed beet red.

"Heh heh. See something interesting in there, did you? What's in my future?" Gunnar had dreamed the previous night about spanking a naked Bryn over his Harley's saddle so he had a pretty good idea what Bryn had seen. *And I fully intend to get that done.* Bryn was already striding across the parking lot and Gunnar jogged to catch him. "You've no idea how many filthy things I plan to do to you." He blew against Bryn's neck. "Focus on that."

Bryn whimpered. "You know I'm wearing tight jeans, right?"

"I am very aware of that, yes."

When they crossed the threshold of the psychiatric unit, Gunnar's sensitive nose started working overtime. "I hate hospitals, they stink." He headed for the reception desk. "Disinfectant masking disease. Yuck."

"Sounds gross. I'm glad I don't have your sniffer."

The receptionist gave Gunnar a big smile. "Hi! How can I help you?"

"We have an appointment with Dr. Tolliver."

"Who is right over there." The woman pointed and a white-coated woman hurried toward them.

"Hi, I'm Sonya Tolliver, it's so kind of you to make time to come over here. Call me Sonya."

"I'm Gunnar and this is Bryn," Gunnar said.

"The augur! From a professional point of view, you are fascinating. I apologize in advance if I get too curious. Tell me to back off if that happens, okay?"

"Uh, sure. I hope we can help you out."

"Does your patient know what we're here to do?" Gunnar asked as they followed Sonya down a long corridor.

"Yes, and she's very excited at the possibility she might find out something about herself. It's very frustrating not being able to remember who you are."

"I can imagine," Gunnar agreed.

"Here we are." Sonya took them into a small private room that had been made cheery with flowers and pictures. "This is one of our family waiting rooms. I thought this might be better than a ward. And this is Jane...which is the name we've been using."

A young woman rose from a chair. She was a redhead, her face colored on one side by fading bruises.

Some of her hair had been shaved and there was a stark scar on her scalp.

"Please sit down, ma'am," Gunnar said, helping her back to her seat. "We won't keep you long."

Bryn sat next to her. He took off his gloves. "Hi, I'm Bryn. Pleased to meet you." He took off his dark glasses and there were two gasps as he revealed his eyes.

"Oh, wow. You can really do this!" Sonya said. "I was a bit skeptical, I have to admit."

"I really can," Bryn said before turning to Jane. "Is it okay if I take your hand?"

"Sure."

Gunnar never failed to be impressed by how Bryn could put a subject at ease. He made sure he wasn't threatening, was polite and friendly. *It's a total personality switch.*

Bryn grasped Jane's hand and wrist then closed his eyes. "Okay, it's a bit misty. She's walking down the aisle on the left of someone whose arm is linked with hers. I assume it's a male from the jacket. It's gray. White shirt. Gold cufflink."

"Where are they?" Gunnar asked.

"Not a church. It's outside, sunny. Her arms are bare so I assume it's warm. There's a kind of pagoda thing at the end of a red carpet and the groom is waiting for her, smiling. Behind the pagoda, I can see the ocean."

"Can you describe the groom?"

"Dark hair, beard and mustache. Wearing formal dark trousers, a white shirt and a bright floral waistcoat. The minister behind him is female. Short gray hair, robes. Jane is happy, excited, looking at the guests to either side of the aisle."

"Can you describe anyone?"

"No. She's looking but not seeing. All her focus is on the groom. Wait. He mouths I love you, Susan or Suzanna, not sure." Bryn released his grip then put his gloves back on. "You had a beautiful wedding, Susan or Suzanna."

"How about we go with Suzie?" Gunnar said. "Cover all bases."

"Suzie's good," the patient said. "I can't believe you saw all that."

"Your strongest memory," Bryn said. "Unfortunately, I can't tell how long ago it was."

Dr Tolliver sat next to Suzie. "Bryn has given us a lot to go on. It won't be long before we find out who you are."

"Our colleague will pass everything on to your police liaison," Gunnar said. "It should be enough."

"Thank you so much," Suzie said. "You have no idea what this means to me."

"Our pleasure. We should be going but, Doc, you let us know if you get any more forgetful patients, okay?"

"I will." The doctor shook Gunnar's hand and then Bryn's. "I understand the need for the gloves. That's quite the talent you have."

Bryn slid his glasses into place. "Pleasure."

"We can find our own way out," Gunnar said. "Let us know when you have news. We don't always get to hear how cases end up."

"I will."

Gunnar called Emmett as soon as they were beyond the door. When he ended the call, he and Bryn strolled down the corridor toward the exit. "How are you doing?" Bryn was even paler than normal.

"I could use a snack and some Tylenol."

"There's a vending machine over there. I spotted it on the way in." Gunnar extracted a blister pack of tablets from his pocket. He popped two out, tipping them into Bryn's hand. "Here you go. We can get a water from the machine too." Bryn chugged the pills dry. "Or you could do that." Gunnar examined the contents of the machine. "They have granola bars, protein snacks…"

"I'll take a Snickers, a Kit-Kat and a packet of double-stuff Oreos. Please. Ooh, and a can of Blue Bottle chilled coffee!"

"Good grief." Gunnar pressed the required buttons and delivered the haul. He got a granola bar for himself. They lingered inside the building while they ate and Bryn swigged his coffee.

"That's better. I hope they find out who Suzie is, she seemed nice."

"Yeah. You got plenty of clues from her memory. Any detective with a brain cell should be able to track her identity down in no time."

"I wish we had more cases like this."

"Better than the usual assorted psychos."

"Yeah." Bryn finished his snacks. He dropped the wrappers in the nearest trash can. "I guess we should get back."

They'd gone fewer than twenty paces outside when the sharp crack of a gunshot echoed through the air. Chips of stone spat from the ground next to Bryn. Gunnar dropped, pulling Bryn with him.

"Down!"

"Fuck!" Bryn gave him a panicked glance.

Gunnar surveyed their position. It was farther back to the building than to get to the first row of cars in the parking lot. He pointed at the nearest car. "Keep low."

Crouching down, Bryn scuttled over to the car with Gunnar close behind him. Another shot took out the car's wing mirror, which exploded with a spray of glass shards. Gunnar dragged Bryn to the other side of the vehicle. He scanned the surrounding buildings and a caught a brief glint of light from a rooftop. "Shooter's over there. We need to get more obstacles between us and him."

"Yeah." Bryn had a hand pressed against his cheek. Blood oozed from between his fingers.

"You're hit!"

"No. Piece of mirror caught me. Nothing serious."

"Okay. You stay behind me and we'll make our way to the back of the lot." They crawled and crouched their way through three rows of cars but they were beginning to thin out and there was less cover. "Lie flat. I'm calling this in." Gunnar made sure that his body was always between Bryn and the shooter's position then made the call. No one else had emerged from the building and he couldn't catch any more flashes of light. "I think he's gone but we don't move until the cops have cleared the rooftops. Let me look at your face."

Bryn rolled onto his back then took his hand away from his cheek. "Stings a bit. I pulled the shard out."

"I don't think it'll need stitching. It's messy but not too deep. Those shades of yours may have saved an eye."

"You think this is The Hammer's doing?"

"I don't want to jump to conclusions but yeah, probably. I also don't think the shooter was trying to kill you, or me for that matter. We were completely exposed when we came out of that building. I think he was a very good shot and those bullets hit exactly where he planned. It's a message."

"Most people send a fucking email."

"Yeah. They do."

Bryn sat with his back to a car door and Gunnar sat next to him. Distant sirens grew closer.

"It'll be okay." Gunnar attempted reassurance.

"Will it?"

Gunnar locked eyes with Bryn. The world around them faded away, leaving just the two of them. He reached out and brushed a stray lock of dark hair from Bryn's eyes. "Is this okay?" he asked, his voice barely above a whisper. Bryn nodded.

Without another word, Gunnar cupped Bryn's face, pulling him closer, and their lips met in a lingering, gentle kiss. Gunnar drew back but Bryn chased him, demanding more. Gunnar got rougher, grazing Bryn's cheek with his stubble. He rested his forehead against Bryn's. "Not quite the location I had in mind for our first kiss, but hey, whatever works."

"I got blood on you."

"My ass is wet and there's a bit of gravel sticking in it."

Bryn burst out laughing. He leaned his head on Gunnar's shoulder. "It was still good. Really good."

"Yeah. Yeah, it was."

Chapter Sixteen

Bryn awoke with a yawn and long stretch. When he checked the time he saw it was almost ten. The previous day had turned into a long drag waiting for the cops to do their work at the hospital. It took manpower to clear the surrounding buildings though eventually it had been confirmed that Gunnar had spotted the correct location for the sniper. The cops found bullet casings and scuff marks showing someone had been there recently. There hadn't been any attempt to conceal the evidence. *Was it really only yesterday he kissed me? The one bright spot in a shitty afternoon. That kiss. Wow.* Bryn's cock responded at the thought and he touched his lips before heading for the shower to deal with it. *Wish Gunnar was here to help.*

Dressed and dry, he went to find his partner. Gunnar was in the office at his computer and Emmett was there too. Bryn paused at the door, enjoying the comforting, familiar scene.

"Good morning, sleepyhead. How are you doing this morning?" Gunnar rose from his seat. He'd left his hair down and Bryn's thoughts strayed to what it might feel like to run his hands through it.

"Hey, are you in there?"

"Just daydreaming. Thanks for letting me sleep in."

"Hmm, thought you might have picked up a concussion I didn't spot yesterday. You needed the rest and you're not that late." Gunnar walked across to him and peered into his eyes. "Have you eaten?"

"No, not yet."

"I put a box of donuts in the kitchen," Emmett said. "They're from Kane's."

Bryn was already moving. Emmett had bought a box of twelve and there were two of the honey-dip kind. "These are mine." Bryn snagged both of them. Gunnar gave an amused shake of his head.

"That is not an appropriate breakfast."

"You can make me pancakes if you want to," Bryn said around a mouthful of sticky goodness.

"Sure. Pancakes are never a bad idea." Gunnar got busy mixing batter then cooked up a huge stack of pancakes.

"Not sure I can eat all those." Bryn eyed the teetering pile. "But I'll give it a go."

"They aren't all for you, mister." Gunnar pulled maple syrup from a cupboard. "Emmett, you want pancakes?"

"Yes please!" the call came back.

Gunnar divided the treats between three plates, taking the biggest portion for himself. He and Bryn had started eating when Emmett arrived, clutching his laptop.

"Don't think you'll need that in here," Bryn said. "It'll get sticky."

"I think I've got it!" Emmett shifted his weight from one foot to the other.

"Got what?" Bryn put more syrup on his pancakes.

"The kill site!"

"For the Walmart killer?"

"Yes!"

"Sit down, Emmett, and tell us what you've found," Gunnar said, "before you have an aneurysm."

"I...yes, of course."

"Take a breath." Bryn carried on eating.

"Sorry, I'm excited. You know I was working on the symbol you sketched, Bryn? I've had to fit it in between other jobs, so it took a while but...I thought I'd look at it from a different angle. The killer is obsessed with historical murderers, isn't he? So I thought, what if his kill site is also historical. I started looking for older interpretations of the symbol and found out that smugglers often used secret signs to mark safe houses, warn fellow smugglers, or indicate the presence of contraband goods. The signs were typically simple and discreet, so they wouldn't attract unwanted attention."

"Okay, interesting." Gunnar paused with a loaded fork halfway to his mouth.

"Isn't it? So apparently smugglers would use chalk to draw symbols on walls or trees. For instance, a circle could indicate a safe house, while a cross might warn of danger. In some cases, they would carve or paint symbols like arrows pointing in a specific direction."

"I saw an arrow in a circle," Bryn said.

"Circles indicated safety, so the symbol you saw probably meant a safe direction."

"This is all great, Emmett, but how does this get us to the kill site?"

"I started looking into Boston's smuggling history. Did you know that there are a ton of tunnels under Boston?"

"Other than the ones with roads in them, no," Bryn admitted.

"Well, there are old tunnels in Boston's North End, often referred to as smugglers' tunnels or pirate tunnels, which connect the wharves to basements of houses and other locations. The Old North Church also conceals a labyrinth of tunnels — secret routes that were crucial to the colonial resistance."

"Wow." Bryn pushed his plate away.

"That's not all. There are also tunnels under Boston Common that were used for covert operations and troop movements during the Revolutionary War. There are others too, but I focused on those that aren't open to the public either for safety or preservation reasons. They include the ones under the Common. I dug into archived pictures from before they were sealed and found this." Emmett swiveled his laptop around. His screen displayed a black and white photo which showed a section of tunnel. On the wall was painted an arrow in a circle.

"Holy fuck, that's it!" Bryn said. "You're a miracle worker, Emmett."

"I just made the links, anyone could have found this. There are maps of the old tunnels too. The killer must have broken in through a sealed entrance or something."

"And you know where this exact piece of tunnel is?" Gunnar asked. Emmett nodded. "Get the information over to the feds right away. Great work!"

Emmett took his laptop and rushed away.

"We're not going to look for the tunnel?" Bryn asked.

"No. It's not our case and this will take manpower. We need to leave Bell and his team to it. I'm sure he'll let us know if they find anything."

"The more I think about it, the more certain I am that the killer must be somebody who works at the store. He must have balls of steel to buy stuff from there but he picked a new cashier. Betty-Jo had only been working there a few days and with that hooded top too, she wouldn't have recognized him. Staff around her were busy and concentrating on their customers."

"Or he doesn't have normal emotions. If they've narrowed down the list of possible suspects, I could read them all. I feel really guilty about Betty-Jo's death, Gunnar. I want to do something."

"I'll make the offer, but let's wait and see what they find at the kill site. Forensics might give them a slam dunk."

"Let's hope. Emmett never got any pancakes and he really deserves some."

"I'll whip up a fresh batch. You can never have too many."

The rest of the morning and early afternoon passed without incident but there was a sense of growing anticipation in their shared office even as they planned their next cases to accept. It was almost three when Gunner's cell rang. "It's Bell." He connected the call and put it on speaker. "Hey, Bell, I hope you've got good news for us. You're on speaker talking to me, Bryn and Emmett."

"If I had my way I'd be poaching Emmett for our office right now. He was spot on with the location and that place is a goldmine of evidence. The entrance was well hidden and chained closed. The killer had even taken the trouble to use an old-looking padlock and chain but there were telltale marks of usage around the keyhole. Once we got inside — and I have to tell you that place is the stuff of horror movies — we found a wider section of tunnel about three hundred yards in. There was a portable table covered in kit. Ropes, knives, surgical gloves… The stuff he bought at the market, which by the way we think he used either to make cut wounds hurt more, with the salt or lemon juice, or to attempt healing with the honey. He may have used that one himself rather than on his victims if he had a wound that he didn't want to show to a doctor or buy stuff from the chemist that might incriminate him further down the line."

"But he wasn't there, I'm guessing?" Bryn said.

"No, he wasn't. We'll put a watch on the entrance, close it up again, in case he comes back once forensics have finished, but the media caught wind of what we were doing and it'll be all over the papers and the internet by now. We'd managed to keep the links between the killings quiet but it's going to come out sooner or later."

"If it does, he'll bolt," Gunnar said.

"Yeah, which is why I have a favor to ask."

"We may be ahead of you if your request is for Bryn to read your suspects. He already suggested it."

"Are you sure you can't read minds?" Bell asked. "That is what I was going to request from Warden. If you're okay with it, I'll let him know. Gotta go through the right channels and he's not a man I want to piss off."

"You want us to come to you?"

"That would be easiest. We'll bring them all in. If they're innocent it should be a case of truth reading but if anyone resists, then we may have to ask Bryn to look at memory and future intent as well."

"Anything that gets this guy caught is good with me," Bryn said.

"In that case, let me make a call to Warden and I'll see you in…let's say an hour. I'll set things in motion to get the suspects brought here. None of them live that far away but we may need to track some of them down if they don't answer our calls."

He ended the call and Bryn made eye contact with Gunnar. "We have to be close, right?"

"The net is definitely drawing in. Let's hope this guy doesn't run before we get him."

Ten minutes later, Warden joined them. He glanced at Bryn, who was occupying his beanbag. "We could get another desk in here, you know."

"I'm good," Bryn said.

"Hmm. I know you've already spoken to Special Agent Bell. To his credit, he made an official request which I'm happy to approve, so get your butts over to the FBI. Take a car, Gunnar. I don't want Bryn on the back of your bike until we're sure you're not gonna get taken out by a sniper. I don't want to be scraping either of you off the asphalt. Emmett, you can go too. It'll be good experience. Also, if anyone over there offers you a job, the answer is no."

"Yes, sir, I mean, no, sir… I mean…" Emmett was pink and flustered. Warden gave him a slow, wolfish smile.

"Get to work, gentlemen. You have a killer to catch."

* * * *

Agent Bell had secured a private room and had already managed to bring in seven of his ten suspects, who'd been seated in a separate room. Bryn was a little nervous about reading so many people in quick succession but it wouldn't be the first time. He made sure Gunnar was within reach.

"I've decided on a change of tack for these interviews," Bell said. "Rather than asking about the victims, I propose to assess knowledge of the kill site. The reason for that is to ensure that on the off chance we have a copycat, or two killers working together, this will save time. Only the killer or killers will know details about the tunnel."

"Do you have reason to believe there is more than one person involved?" Gunnar asked.

"Not at this time, I'm being cautious."

"Why have the people we're seeing today landed on the shortlist?"

"Either because they have no alibi for the dates the victims were taken, or their alibis are sketchy for one or more of them."

"Fair enough. What about the ones who aren't here yet?"

"Efforts are being made to track them down. They may have arrived before Bryn gets to the end of this first bunch. I should also say, Bryn, if you need a break, you only have to say."

"Keep the coffee coming, Bell."

"He'll take a break after the first three," Gunnar said. "He'll need a snack."

"I will?"

"You will. Non-negotiable."

Bell grinned. "Are they like this all the time, Emmett?"

"They are and then some," Emmett replied before ducking his head. "I shouldn't have said that, should I?"

"We love you, Emmett. Never change," Gunnar reassured him. "Shall we get started?"

Over the next three hours, Bryn gradually eliminated all the suspects. Only one man had any knowledge of the Boston tunnels and he was an amateur history buff. He didn't recognize the symbol on the wall and had never been inside any of the tunnels.

One of the three missing suspects had turned up under his own steam. He had a numb face from a dental appointment but was relieved to be able to clear his name.

Finally, it was only the small team left. Bell organized for Chinese food to be delivered.

Bryn didn't wait for anyone else. He poked into boxes and claimed a portion of mushroom rice and some prawn curry. "So hungry!"

Gunnar held back but Bell had made provision for a wolf-sized appetite and had been generous. Soon everyone was eating.

"Who are we missing, Bell?"

"The two managers. Drake Romano who runs the store and Dave Frederics, the security manager."

"We met both of them when we went to view their security footage," Gunnar said.

"Any concerns about either of them?"

"Not at the time, but we weren't there long. They were cooperative. The manager didn't stay with us 'cos he had to haul some kid out of a freezer."

"I'm not going to ask…"

"So where are they?"

"Romano is at the store and had to arrange cover, but should be here soon. Frederics didn't show up for work this morning. I have people out looking for him."

"So without jumping to conclusions, that doesn't look good for him, does it?"

"Can't say that it does."

"That place is bristling with cameras. He's in an ideal job to see everything and everyone. He'd definitely know how to avoid cameras and his build fits the profile." Gunnar tried not to get too excited that they might have found their killer. "Did he have an alibi at all?"

"No. He isn't in a relationship. Lives alone and says that at the times the victims were taken, he was either at home or working. He can produce witnesses that he was at work but no one has eyes on him all the time and part of his role is to walk the premises, including the parking lot, at regular intervals. He could have disappeared for hours during a working day and anyone who noticed he'd gone would assume he was working someplace else."

"I guess the same applies to the manager," Bryn said. "He must have off-site meetings."

"He's a similar character. No family to speak of and not very social. Belongs to a gun club but doesn't go to the range very often. Members we found who know him didn't have anything negative to say, though."

"Neither of them are obvious psychos," Bryn said.

"They never are." Bell munched on a spring roll.

A young staffer poked her head around the door. "Agent Bell. Mr. Romano has arrived."

"Put him in the waiting room while we get the room cleared, Menaz. I'll come get him myself when we're ready."

The remains of the meal were hurriedly cleared away and after a quick comfort break, they were ready.

"How's your head?" Gunnar asked Bryn.

"Still attached."

"You need water?"

"I'm good. Let's get this over with."

Romano was brought in and Bell gave him the same introduction to proceedings as he'd given the others.

"Got it. And apologies for not being able to get here sooner. I had to find a deputy to cover for me at the store and there's a flu bug going around. It took a while."

"Not a problem. You're here now."

"Yeah, but I want this all sorted out as much as you do. If this gets you closer to catching Betty-Jo's killer, I don't want to delay anything."

Bryn took Romano's wrist and nodded that he was ready to begin.

Bell cleared his throat. "Are you aware of the tunnels beneath Boston Common?"

"Yes." Romano spoke without hesitation.

"Truth."

"How do you know about them?"

"Dave Frederics told me about them."

"Truth."

Gunnar and Bell exchanged looks.

"What exactly did he tell you about them?"

"He said he had found an old entrance to one of the tunnels. He'd done some research on the web and wanted to take a look, so he did. I think he hoped to find historical stuff that might have been left down there."

"Truth."

"Do you know if he got inside?"

"Yes, he did. He showed me pictures."

"When was this?" Bell didn't wait for Bryn to confirm the truth of that statement.

"Uh, I can't be sure, but I'd say it was around eighteen months ago."

"Truth."

"I'm going to show you a picture, Mr. Romano. It's a drawing of a symbol and I want you to tell me if you've seen it." Bell pushed the sketch across the table.

Romano looked at it. "It kinda looks like something that was on the wall of the tunnel. Dave thought it might be an old smugglers' mark. He was fascinated by the historical connection."

"Truth."

"Do you think Frederics has been into the tunnels again?"

"Can't say. I would guess so, because he got really into Boston's history after that, but I don't absolutely know."

"Also true." Bryn's hand was shaking. He closed his eyes, the strain of what he was doing evident.

"Bryn needs to take a break," Gunnar said.

Bell nodded. "We have what we need for now, Mr. Romano. If you'd be so kind as to go with one of my agents, they'll take a statement from you. Anything you can remember from your conversations with Dave Frederics would be helpful."

"Am I going to need a new security manager?" Romano asked as he stood.

"That remains to be seen, but if he turns up at work or contacts you in any way, you need to let us know immediately."

"I will." Romano left with the same agent who had announced his arrival.

"I need something sugary for Bryn," Gunnar said.

"Way ahead of you." Emmett extracted three candy bars from his satchel. "I brought these with me, just in case."

"My head hurts," Bryn muttered.

"I'm sure it does. You've done too much again." Gunnar got growly. He thrust a bottle of water into Bryn's hand then unwrapped one of the candy bars. He broke off a piece. "Open."

Bryn opened his mouth, accepting the chocolate Gunnar shoved between his lips. "Hmm, good to know that's one order you respond to," Gunnar whispered, his voice low enough that only Bryn would hear amidst the chatter in the room. Several agents on the investigating team had joined them to hear the results of the readings.

Bryn blinked and gulped. "I'm okay, but I'd like to get back to the apartment so I can take a nap. Is that okay?" He was utterly drained.

"We sure can."

Emmett was already packing his things. "This was fascinating. I'm glad Warden let me come along."

Fifteen minutes later, after saying their goodbyes to Bell and his team, Gunnar, Bryn and Emmett were in the car and heading for home. Emmett took shotgun so that Bryn could get horizontal on the rear seat.

"That was a lot for Bryn to handle today, wasn't it?" Emmett said.

"Yeah. I think it paid off, though."

"Sure sounded like it. I hope Bell tracks the security guy down fast. Do you think he's made a run for it?"

"It wouldn't surprise me. This killer isn't stupid. He'll have a backup plan. He was right there in the security room with us and I didn't pick up anything suspect. He was helpful. Normal. He has to be a sociopath."

Emmett shuddered. "Those poor people. I hate thinking about what he did to them."

"Try to put it out of your head. When it sneaks in, think of something happy."

"Will Bryn have to read Dave Frederics when they catch him?"

"Not if he confesses or if they find enough evidence to convict him without a confession. I can't imagine he thought his kill site would be found so it must be full of forensics. In the image Bryn saw, the killer wasn't wearing gloves."

"That would be good. I'm sure Bryn has enough bad stuff in his head already."

"I'm right here, guys," Bryn spoke from the back seat.

"You should be sleeping," Gunnar snapped. "And he's not wrong."

"True. Are we there yet?"

"You did not just say that!"

Bryn chuckled. "What can I say? I live to make your world a better place."

Chapter Seventeen

It was four days before the team heard any news about Dave Frederics. Agent Bell visited the GRC in person to give them an update so they convened in the conference room. Bryn's ripped black jeans and scuffed boots contrasted with Emmett's latest ensemble of navy chinos paired with a pale blue, diamond-patterned sweater-vest, blue shirt and a fancy yellow bow tie. Gunnar had on his usual faded jeans and a checked flannel shirt with the sleeves rolled up. He'd forgone his bun for a loose ponytail. Bryn found it hard to look at him without drooling. So far, there had been no repeat of the kiss in the hospital parking lot and Bryn was on the verge of drastic action. *Maybe I should walk out of my room naked with a sign around my neck saying 'horny and desperate', that might work.* He held back a sigh and switched his focus to the room.

"Ooh, pastries!" Refreshments had arrived and he hadn't noticed. He reached for a cherry Danish and Emmett circled the table pouring coffee for everyone.

"You should visit more often, Bell. They've rolled out the good stuff for you," Bryn said, munching happily.

"Glad to be of service." Bell took a seat. "I have news. Dave Frederics' body was recovered from a car wreck this morning. It happened near Wareham and he appears to have driven off a bridge into the Agawam River near Route 25. We don't know exactly when, but the ME estimates time of death being the night after we interviewed the Walmart suspects. The car was discovered submerged and overturned in the river. A dive team had to recover the body."

"Did the crash kill him or the water?" Gunnar asked.

"He had head injuries but suspected cause of death is drowning. We'll know for sure after the postmortem."

"So he made a run for it," Bryn said.

"We found his DNA all over the kill site," Bell said. "Though not on any weapons. There weren't any knives there so he could have removed them. We'll keep looking. The only other traces were from three of the victims. Obviously, Betty-Jo was never taken there. I would have preferred to take him to trial."

Bryn nodded. "On to new things then, I suppose."

"Just the paperwork to clear on this one now."

"It's a bit of a letdown, isn't it?" Bryn said. "All that work and we never actually caught him. He caught himself."

"It happens," Gunnar said. "At least we know he won't be hurting anyone else. Is there any news on Everard Templeton, Bell?"

"I'm afraid not. He's vanished into thin air. He was one step ahead of us from the start. I'm convinced he had help, possibly from inside the FBI. You didn't hear that from me."

"He'll show himself eventually," Gunnar said. "He's too arrogant to stay hidden for long."

"Maybe he'll drive off a bridge too." Bryn grabbed another pastry. "That would work for me."

"We'll do our best to find him, Bryn."

"I know you will." *Doesn't mean you'll catch him, though.*

"In the meantime, we have work to do so we'd better get back to it." Gunnar shoved his chair back. "Nice to see you, Bell. Thanks for coming over in person."

Once they were back in the office, Bryn found it hard to settle. "You were quiet down there, Emmett. Anything wrong?"

"Oh…no. It's not my place to say."

"Of course it is," Gunnar said. "What's on your mind?"

"Well, I'm probably being silly because I'm not a detective and I don't have much experience with these things but…don't you think Dave Frederics' death was a bit too convenient?"

That piqued Bryn's interest. "What do you mean?"

"Well, it all seems a bit easy for a killer who was so complex. All the history stuff…wouldn't you have thought someone like that would have an escape plan if he thought the net was closing in on him?"

"Sometimes the best answers to puzzles are the simplest ones," Gunnar said. "Don't forget, Frederics' DNA was found at the kill site."

"I know. It's just a feeling. If it's okay with you guys, I'm going to go have lunch with Talbot."

"Of course it is. Are you going out?"

"No, we brown-bagged it today. He wants to show me something he's been working on that might make data links in my filing system easier to set up."

"That sounds...fascinating," Bryn said, pleased at managing to sound sincere.

"You're such a liar, Bryn!" Emmett grabbed his satchel. "I'm going to go play computers and leave the detecting to you guys."

Emmett scurried out of the office. Bryn exchanged a look with Gunnar. "You know, he has good instincts. Maybe this *was* too straightforward."

"Let's think about it. What are the reasons for believing Frederics is the killer? First is opportunity. His job gave him the perfect chances to spot people and take them without him being missed."

Bryn nodded. "Second, he had no alibis for any of the dates that victims went missing, or the night that Betty-Jo was killed."

"Third—he has the right build for the person you read in the checkout line."

"True, but all of those things could equally be applied to Drake Romano."

"They could. So consider the evidence from truth reading Romano today. We know that Frederics had an interest in the tunnels, that he found an entrance and went inside. The picture he took of the symbol on the wall proves he was in the section used as the kill site and his DNA was found all over the place down there."

"Yeah. It's pretty damning." Bryn frowned. "But...it also gave Romano a reason for knowing about the tunnels and recognizing the symbol. It's possible he went there too, if Frederics told him exactly where the entrance was, and Bell didn't specifically ask him that question."

"Now I think about it, Bell didn't ask Romano anything that would incriminate him. His answers pointed everything at Frederics." Gunnar paced the office. "You were exhausted and we stopped the questions thinking we had enough."

"Sorry."

"Not your fault at all. We could have kept Romano there, asked him more after you'd eaten and rested. We didn't."

"But the DNA...are we reaching for something that isn't there?"

"Maybe, but you saw a bare hand on a knife and no knives have been found. Let's have some lunch and think on it some more. How about grilled cheese and tomato soup?"

"Yes please! My housemother made that whenever anyone was sick or feeling down."

"It's a great American tradition, plus it involves cheese and therefore has to be good."

Within half an hour they were sitting at the table eating. "This makes me stupidly happy," Bryn said, scraping the last of the soup from his dish.

"Sometimes the simple things make all the difference." Gunnar crunched the remaining crust from his second grilled cheese.

"As simple as a kiss?"

"Yeah. As simple as that." It seemed like Gunnar might say something else but before he could, Emmett burst into the kitchen closely followed by Talbot.

"We need to tell you something!"

"I'd never have known," Gunnar said. "Sit down both of you. Breathe."

"This is a really nice place." Talbot looked around, wide-eyed. "Can I smell grilled cheese?"

"You can," Gunnar said with a grin.

"Talbot!" Emmett exclaimed. "Focus!"

Talbot blinked. "Sorry, yes…we did a thing." He put his laptop on the table.

"A thing?" Bryn asked.

"We were messing around with code," Emmett said. "Talbot was showing me some of the things he's been learning how to do and he showed me this anagram generator he made. You put letters into it and it comes up with all possible combinations of letters. We used all our names. Bryn Ashton can be Anny Throbs."

Talbot giggled. "Gunnar Ericson could be Caring Neurons."

"That's better than mine," Bryn muttered.

"Yeah, anyway…we put in the Walmart manager's name. One of the options for Drake Romano is Aaron Mordke."

"I'm not following, Emmett. Is that supposed to be significant?"

"I recognized the name from somewhere, so we did a search. Aaron Mordke Kosminski was a Polish Jewish immigrant who lived in London and has been named as one of the primary suspects in the Jack the Ripper case."

Talbot took up the story. "Jack the Ripper was responsible for a series of brutal murders in the Whitechapel district of London in 1888, targeting women, particularly prostitutes, and mutilating their bodies in grotesque ways. Despite extensive investigation, the identity of the Ripper has never been proved.

"Kosminski was born in Poland in 1865 and immigrated to London with his family, settling in the Whitechapel area. He worked as a barber, and by the late 1880s, he'd developed significant mental health issues, which apparently led to his being put in an asylum in 1891. He suffered from paranoid schizophrenia and displayed erratic behavior, including a deep mistrust of women and violent tendencies.

"Kosminski became a suspect because he was around the area and because he matched descriptions provided by witnesses. But there was no hard evidence at the time linking him to the crimes, and the police never formally charged him."

Emmett bounced in his seat. "Recently, interest in Kosminski as a suspect reignited because in 2014, a shawl said to belong to one of the Ripper's victims, Catherine Eddowes, was tested for DNA. The tests allegedly found a match to Kosminski's family line, suggesting he may have been the killer. The evidence has been heavily disputed by experts but...well, Jack the Ripper remains a mystery. It can't be a coincidence, can it? Kosminski could have gotten away with a series of brutal killings."

Gunnar drummed his fingers on the table. "No, it can't. It's an obscure enough connection to fit with a man who thinks his intellect is superior to anyone else's."

"He sat in that room at the FBI and didn't as much as twitch," Bryn said.

Gunnar got to his feet. "Emmett, call Agent Bell and tell him everything you've told us. Let him know we're on our way to Walmart. This fucker needs to answer a lot more questions."

"I'm coming too," Bryn said. He got a hard look from Gunnar. "You'll need me to read him, won't you?"

"Fine. But you wear a bulletproof vest and do exactly as I tell you to."

"Nothing new there then."

Gunnar was nowhere near certain that taking Bryn with him was a good idea but arguing about it would have taken far too long. As they drove to the store, he kept his focus on the road. The thick drizzle made everything gray and the traffic was sluggish. He'd been tempted to take the Harley but didn't want to make Bryn even more of a target than he already was.

"Do you think Emmett's right?" Bryn asked, fiddling with the straps on his bulletproof vest.

"Yeah, I do. The more I think about it, that car crash was far too convenient."

"How do you want to approach this?"

"I think we go in and say we need to take a look at Dave Frederics' office. Tying up loose ends, that kind of thing. Then we have a reason to check in with Romano and you can read him."

"Okay. You want memory or future intent, because there won't be time for both if he realizes what I'm up to?"

"Memory. If he's our perp, his strongest memory is most likely to be one of the murders. Then we'll know for certain."

"Okay."

Gunnar pulled into the parking lot and they both got out of the car. "It's busy in there, if the number of vehicles here is anything to go by. We need to be careful."

"What do you mean?" Bryn stared at the store.

"If he in anyway suspects why we're here, we can't put members of the public at risk. If he thinks he's cornered, he might get violent. No confrontation in the main store area."

"Right."

The piercing wail of a fire alarm sounded across the parking lot and for a moment everyone froze. Shoppers paused mid-stride, heads turning toward the Walmart entrance. Then, the doors opened and people poured out in a chaotic stream. A mother half-dragged, half-carried her crying toddler, while a teenager sprinted past, glancing back over his shoulder. An elderly man shuffled slowly, his cane tapping, assisted by a young store employee. The automatic doors struggled to keep up, sliding open and shut as people flooded through them. A garbled loudspeaker announcement fought against the alarm's screech, but it was impossible to decipher.

"Not a coincidence, right?" Bryn said as he and Gunnar walked toward the store.

"Nope. He must have been watching the security feeds and saw us arrive. This isn't good."

A small group of onlookers had gathered in the middle of the parking lot. Some speculated on the cause of the alarm, while others stood, phones held up, recording everything. A man in a baseball cap shook his head as he scrolled through his social media feed, muttering, "This'll be all over the goddam news in ten minutes."

Gunnar couldn't see any smoke coming from the building—at least, not yet. A woman in a Walmart vest came past, guiding a cluster of employees to a designated meeting point. "Keep moving, everyone. Gather over there, please."

Gunnar flashed his badge at her. "Is this a drill, ma'am?"

"No, sir. No drills planned for today."

"Thanks." Gunnar placed a quick call to Emmett and asked him to contact the fire service to let them know that all might not be as it seemed. The crowd of evacuated shoppers swelled, spreading across the lot. Those lingering too close to the entrance were nudged along. When the stream of people trickled to a halt, the store's entrance stood empty. Gunnar showed his badge again outside the doors. "We suspect a crime is in progress. Keep everyone away from the store."

Inside the store, the fluorescent lights overhead flickered, casting a cold glow over the aisles. Abandoned shopping carts stood all over the place.

"It's like one of those movies where everyone dies then they all turn into zombies," Bryn muttered. "I don't smell smoke, do you?"

"No."

"It's creepy as hell in here."

Gunnar grunted in agreement. Shelves loomed high on either side, creating canyons. "We'll head to the staff door we went through before."

"He's probably watching us."

They reached the back of the store where the staff door stood open. A faint noise — something between a scrape and a shuffle — came from somewhere ahead.

"Let's go," Gunnar said. "Stay behind me."

Gunnar approached with caution but both the security office and Romano's office were empty, as were the staff break room, supplies closet and restrooms. There was no sign of anyone. At the end of a corridor there was another door. Gunnar nudged it open with his foot and discovered it led to the store's warehouse. The lights were off and rows of racking stacked with boxes stretched into the gloom.

Bryn found the torch app on his cell and aimed the beam ahead of them. From somewhere ahead, a metallic clang reverberated through the space. Bryn swung the beam in the direction of the sound as Gunnar drew his weapon.

"We know you're in here, Romano. Show yourself!" Gunnar shouted. For a moment, there was nothing — just the faint hum of refrigerated stores — then a shadow shifted about halfway down the aisle near a gap in the shelving.

"Don't move!" Gunnar barked.

Romano stepped into the wavering beam of light. He held a trembling woman, no older than thirty, her face streaked with tears. He had a hunting knife pressed to her throat. She whimpered, clutching at Romano's restraining arm, her terror evident.

"Don't come any closer, Detective."

Gunnar froze. He kept his gun steady. Bryn tried to remember to breathe. "Okay," Gunnar said, his voice calm, measured. "Let's talk. Nobody needs to get hurt here."

Romano laughed. "Don't give me that crap. She's the insurance that gets me out of here. You know I'll slice her throat if I have to."

"He's giving me serious evil villain vibes right now," Bryn muttered.

"Not getting any closer. Setting off the alarm was clever. You saw us arrive, right?"

"It was a bit of luck being in Dave's office at the right time."

"Did he help you kill those people?"

"That moron? Of course not. He was so soft he let shoplifters go if they returned the goods they stole. Pathetic. How did you work out it was me?"

"Someone a lot cleverer than me unscrambled your name then connected the dots. Is Romano even your real name?"

"Changed it legally years ago. This ain't my first rodeo."

"Christ, how many people has this maniac slaughtered? If he gets away with that woman, she's dead. Fuck, this is a bad idea but..." Bryn stepped forward, his hands raised. "Let her go. You don't need her."

"What the fuck are you doing, Bryn?" Gunnar made a grab for him but Bryn sidestepped him.

"And what? Let your partner shoot me?" Romano said.

"No one's shooting anyone," Bryn said. "You let her go, and I'll take her place."

"Bryn..." Gunnar's voice was low with warning. Bryn didn't look at him—he kept his gaze fixed on Romano.

"You want leverage, right?" Bryn continued. "She's not it. She's terrified, she's no threat to you. But me? I'm worth something. You'll have a better chance of walking out of here if you take me instead."

"Don't do this," Gunnar muttered.

"You have a better idea?" Bryn shot back.

Romano's face twisted into something unreadable. "An augur for this silly bitch seems like a good trade."

With a hard shove, Romano pushed the woman forward. She stumbled, collapsing into Gunnar's arms as Bryn took her place. The knife was pressed to his side now, Romano's arm around his neck.

"Bryn," Gunnar said again, sounding furious.

"I'm fine," Bryn said. "Just get her out of here."

The hostage sobbed quietly as Gunnar guided her to the door. His eyes never left Bryn.

Bryn stood completely still. "You made the right call," he said softly. "Shall we figure out how we both get out of this alive?"

Gunnar guided the store worker through the empty store. Her breathing came in shallow, panicked gasps. "You're okay," he said, "just keep moving. We're almost out."

She nodded but stumbled into an abandoned cart. Gunnar tightened his grip on her arm, steadying her. "Slow breaths," he instructed, glancing over his shoulder to ensure they weren't being followed.

The front entrance came into view, the glow of red and blue lights flashing faintly through the glass doors. When they got outside, the parking lot was alive with activity — uniformed officers bustling everywhere. The woman collapsed to her knees on the asphalt, sobbing uncontrollably. Gunnar crouched beside her, his hand still on her shoulder. "You're safe now," he said gently. "It's over."

"It's not over. He's still in there — your partner...he was so brave."

Gunnar clenched his jaw. Every fiber of his being screamed to get back inside but he forced himself to stay, just long enough to ensure the hostage was out of harm's way.

"Officer!" he barked, waving over a nearby uniformed cop. The officer jogged over. Gunnar checked his name tag. "Take her...Officer Harris," Gunnar said, helping the woman to her feet and handing her off to the officer. "Romano was using her as a hostage. Get her checked out. Are the feds here?"

"Yeah, it's their scene."

"Find Special Agent Bell. Tell him Detective Ericson is in the store and that Romano has his partner. You got that?"

"Got it."

Gunnar wasn't about to abandon Bryn. Gun in hand, he went back into the store and straight through to the warehouse. He walked past Bryn's abandoned bulletproof vest.

"Romano!" Gunnar's voice boomed, amplified by the cavernous space. "You're surrounded. Let Bryn go, and maybe I'll consider not blowing your head off." *Not guaranteeing it, though.*

"Still think you're in control, Detective?" Romano's voice crackled through the warehouse's PA system. The sound echoed and Gunnar froze, scanning the rows of shelves, his gun raised. *He has to be near a fixed phone.*

"You want me to slip my knife between your partner's ribs? You'd be surprised how easily a blade penetrates flesh. The sensation is…satisfying."

The PA system crackled again, but this time it wasn't Romano's voice—it was Special Agent Bell.

"Romano, this is the FBI. Let the hostage go, and we'll talk. The building is surrounded. There's nowhere to go."

Gunnar's sharp ears caught the faintest scuffle—a scrape of boots against concrete, a muffled grunt. Rounding the corner, he caught a glimpse of movement. Romano was dragging Bryn toward a metal staircase that led to a precarious network of catwalks crisscrossing the roof space above the shelving.

Gunnar stepped into full view, holding his gun steady. "Let him go," Gunnar ordered. "Or I'll make sure you regret it."

Romano froze for a heartbeat, then sneered. He yanked Bryn in front of him like a shield, pressing the knife to his throat. "You want to play hero?" Romano barked, dragging Bryn up the staircase in jerky, awkward steps. Bryn struggled violently, twisting his body, refusing to make Romano's progress easy. Each thrash sent tremors through the staircase and the bolts groaned in protest.

Reaching the catwalk, Romano half-turned. "Here's the deal!" he shouted, his voice echoing through the roof space. "I get a fueled car, safe passage out of here and a guarantee I won't be followed. Or..." He tilted his head toward the drop. "I'll toss him over like yesterday's garbage."

Bryn fought harder, apparently unconcerned by Romano's knife. One well-aimed blow landed squarely in Romano's ribs, and he staggered, losing his balance for a split second. The catwalk trembled violently with a screech of straining metal.

Gunnar seized the opening. His finger tightened on the trigger and he fired. The sharp crack of the gunshot split the air, and Romano cried out as the bullet buried itself in his shoulder. His knife clattered to the catwalk before spinning off the edge.

Bryn broke free with a snarl, stumbling to his knees. His momentum carried him dangerously close to the edge and he clawed at the grating to steady himself. Gunnar's heart lurched, but Bryn scrambled to his feet then stepped back from the edge. He gave Gunnar a brief wave then drove his boot into Romano's side. By the time Gunnar reached them, Romano was sprawled on the catwalk, clutching his injured shoulder and whimpering.

"You're done," Gunnar said, slapping a pair of cuffs onto Romano's wrists. He hauled him to his feet with a rough jerk. "Move. You can walk down, or I can shove you over the edge. Your call."

Romano paled, all bluster gone. "I'll walk," he mumbled, wobbling as Gunnar pushed him toward the stairs.

Behind them, Bryn huffed, swiping at his bloodied shirt. "Aw, come on! I was kind of hoping you'd throw him over. The guy ruined my favorite T-shirt when he scratched me." He tugged the fabric up, revealing deep scratches that oozed blood across his side.

A low growl escaped Gunnar's throat. "You call those scratches?" he snapped. "They're a hell of a lot more than that."

Bryn waved him off. "Relax, big guy. Nothing to wolf-out about."

Gunnar didn't answer. His grip tightened on Romano's arm, his jaw clenching. "Let's just get this over with," he muttered, dragging his prisoner down the staircase, already plotting what words he'd have for Bryn once Romano was out of the picture.

When they reached the bottom of the stairs, there was a swarm of FBI agents waiting to take Romano into custody. As the agents led him away, Gunnar leaned against some racking. Bell came over to him.

"You could've waited for backup," he said dryly.

"And miss the chance to take him down? No way. Besides, he took Bryn."

"You know how many things could've gone sideways in here? Bryn could've been killed, *you* could've been killed, and I'd be the one cleaning up the mess. The paperwork would've taken weeks and Warden would've declared war on the FBI."

"Yeah, well…it was worth the risk." He gave Bryn a pointed glare. "If we hadn't acted, Romano might be halfway across the state by now."

"Did you get a read on him, Bryn?" Bell asked.

"Yeah. He's one sick puppy. He enjoyed torturing Hunter Carshaw the most. While we were getting up close and familiar, he also told me he spiked Dave Frederics' coffee with hallucinogens before convincing him he needed to run. The crash was inevitable. Romano did find out about the tunnels from Frederics, that was true, but they were never there together. He convinced Frederics not to go back after replacing the padlock and chain, told him the place was likely being monitored by the city but before that, Frederics had been there several times. He was a convenient fall guy."

"Okay. You guys can take a hike. We've got it from here. We need to get the store reopened because the people outside are getting feral. We'll keep the back offices and warehouse sealed off. I'll come by tomorrow to take statements from both of you."

Gunnar nodded. "Okay." He and Bryn walked back to their car in silence. Gunnar held his tongue until they were inside the vehicle.

"What the hell were you thinking, Bryn? Are you trying to put me in an early grave?"

Bryn sighed, rubbing the back of his neck. "I was thinking about saving the hostage's life."

"And what about *your* life?" Gunnar leaned closer. "You put yourself in the hands of a guy with nothing to lose. Do you know how that could've ended? How close you came to —"

"I know," Bryn cut him off. "I know exactly how close I came. But it worked. She's safe. He's in custody. It's over."

"It's not over for me!" Gunnar snapped. "Have you any idea what it was like for me to leave you with him while I took that woman out of there? Watch you put yourself in that kind of danger and be helpless? That wasn't a trade you needed to make."

"I couldn't just stand there and do nothing."

Gunnar ran a hand through his hair, taking a deep breath to steady himself. "And that's what scares me," he admitted. "You took a risk like your life doesn't matter, but it does. To me, it does."

"You mean that?" Bryn asked, his voice barely above a whisper.

"Every word," Gunnar said.

"Sorry?"

"Don't fucking do it again." And then, before either of them could overthink it, Gunnar grabbed Bryn's T-shirt and pulled him close. Their lips met in a fierce, desperate kiss, all the tension, fear, and heightened emotion from the day melting away.

When they finally broke apart, both breathless, Bryn grinned. "Now, are you done yelling at me?"

"Not even close," Gunnar murmured. "Let's get out of here."

"You're the boss."

"Maybe you could try to remember that."

Epilogue

"I should put you two under house arrest," Warden said. "Of all the idiotic... Do either of you have *any* sense of self-preservation?"

"It was my fault," Bryn said, sitting up a bit straighter in his seat at the conference room table. "It just kinda came into my head that I needed to do something. There's no doubt Romano would have killed that woman."

"But you didn't think it was possible he might kill *you*? The GRC's most valuable asset."

"Well...no. I knew Gunnar would find a way to rescue me, I just had to stay alive long enough for him to work out how."

Gunnar stared at him. Warden shook his head. "You two raise my blood pressure to stratospheric levels, you know that? No, don't say anything else. You." He pointed at Bryn. "You ever do something like that again and I will personally cane your ass. And you." It was Gunnar's turn. "You should know better."

"I think I should be calling human resources," Bryn muttered. "That kind of sanction can't be in the staff handbook."

"There's a special fucking chapter written just for you. Don't push me."

Bryn pouted. "So not fair."

"We'll put a line under this fiasco and be thankful that neither of you ended up in the mortuary. The FBI is very pleased with yesterday's result and Romano is singing like a canary. He's talking about fifteen other killings across four states. Seems to be proud of not being caught for so long."

"Jesus, what a nut job," Bryn said.

"Quite. What he said to you about drugging Frederics was also true, Bryn. The autopsy showed cause of death was drowning but there were massive amounts of LSD in his system. That stuff works within one to four hours and the effects can go on for up to twelve, so the Lord only knows what he was seeing when he drove off that bridge."

"The fifth Boston victim then," Gunnar said.

"Indeed." Warden leaned back in his chair. "I have other news. Salvatore Russo has left the country. The feds tracked his private jet to Colombia last night. They believe he'll wait for the dust to settle following the accountant's trial before returning."

"That'll give him time to cook up more ways to get to Bryn," Gunnar said.

"Possibly, but for now, he's out of your hair and has plenty of other things to worry about."

"So just an escaped maniac and half the criminal underworld to look out for then," Bryn said. "That's a relief."

"You can both take the rest of today off to have a break. No going out. You can go, Bryn. Emmett has been frantic with worry so go reassure him that you'll try to develop some common sense."

"Yes, boss." Bryn slunk out of the room, closing the door behind him.

Gunnar eyed Warden. "I take full responsibility for what happened yesterday. I put Bryn in that situation."

"I don't hold grudges, Gunnar, and he's as culpable as you. It's done. The most revealing thing out of all of this is that he trusts you completely. I was right to bring you in."

"You mean *you* asked for me? I wasn't suggested?"

"That's right." Warden steepled his fingers.

"Wait a goddamn minute..." Lightbulbs flashed in Gunnar's brain. "You're a fucking augur, aren't you?"

"Not quite, and my abilities are at nothing like the level Bryn's are. I have occasional glimpses of the future. In my dreams."

"And you saw me?"

"I saw the two of you, together. Let's leave it at that."

"I...got nothing. You didn't think it was worth telling me this sooner?"

"It would have made no difference. There's no need to tell Bryn."

Gunnar's head hurt.

"Also, I need to let you know about something else that I'd rather he not hear about yet."

Gunnar's stomach knotted. "Templeton?"

"Yes. Another letter arrived here yesterday."

"Fuck. He knows where we work."

"A succinct summary of the situation, Detective."

"What did it say?"

"'I haven't forgotten you. See you soon, Everard.'"

"How does he manage to make a few words sound so threatening?"

"It's a talent. Same paper and ink as before. The handwriting matches. It was mailed from Dallas, Texas, though that doesn't mean he's there."

"It would be nice if he is that far away, but he's probably nowhere near there."

"No, but the FBI are on it. Someone mailed the letter, even if it wasn't him."

"So…what's next?"

"We carry on working. You and Bryn continue the excellent work you've been doing and I will focus some of our resources on tracking down Dr. Templeton."

"But not us?"

"No. There are too many cases that need your attention. Templeton will reveal himself in time. He, or one of his allies, will inevitably make a mistake."

Gunnar wasn't convinced but there wasn't much he could do about it. "Okay. I won't tell Bryn. He already knows Templeton wants him. He doesn't need a reminder."

"No, he doesn't. You can go now. You've earned a few hours off."

As he climbed the stairs to the top floor, Gunnar wondered if Warden ever took time off. *That was quite the revelation about what he can do but I should have worked that out sooner. Why would he be in charge of this place without some personal understanding of what it's like to have gene abilities? It makes sense.* He found Bryn and Emmett in the kitchen. Emmett, puffy-eyed, was clutching a plate of cookies while Bryn made coffee.

"Hey, Emmett, you okay?" Gunnar asked.

"I am now. I was so worried. Agent Bell kept calling with updates and when he told me what was going on,

I felt horrible. It's my fault you had to go after Drake Romano and you could have been killed. I couldn't concentrate on anything even though I knew you were safe."

"You are absolutely not at fault here, Emmett," Gunnar said.

"I already told him that," Bryn contributed. "We decided coffee and cookies were needed."

"Sounds good." Gunnar took a sniff of the cookies. "Honey and stem ginger."

"You'd better bring the tin, Emmett, or we won't get a look-in." Bryn poured coffee into three mugs. "Where honey is concerned, you'd think he was a bear, not a wolf."

Emmett frowned. "You think there are any ursines out there?"

"Not that I know of," Bryn said. "And I've seen plenty of gene-affected people, but who knows. Never say never."

"I kinda like the idea. Bears have the cutest fluffy ears."

"And massive claws," Gunnar chimed in, getting a baleful look from Emmett. "Sorry."

They took their drinks and cookies through to the couch. "Warden gave us the rest of the day off," Gunnar said. "Which means you've got the day off too, Emmett."

"Me? Really?" Emmett munched a cookie.

"Of course. You work just as hard as we do."

"It would be nice to go do some shopping for the apartment... Not that we don't like your stuff, Gunnar, but Talbot and me want to add some homey touches of our own."

"Then you should do that."

"What are you guys going to do?" Emmett asked.

"Use the gym in the basement, maybe. Catch up on some personal admin, that kind of thing," Gunnar said. "Order in later."

"Sounds way too productive," Bryn said. "I'm having a bubble bath then vegging in front of the TV. I need to catch up on all the daytime dramas."

Emmett swallowed the last of his coffee. "Well, have fun. I'm glad you're not dead. I'll see you in the morning." He grabbed another cookie before he left.

"That boy has zero social skills," Gunnar said. "Though I'm glad we're not dead too." He flopped onto the sofa next to Bryn.

"If Everard Templeton or Salvatore Russo get their way that might change."

"Both problems for another day," Gunnar said.

"You know what I want right now?" Bryn said.

"Tell me."

"You've kissed me twice and both times have not been in the most romantic circumstances. I want you to kiss me again. Right here. Right now."

"Oh, you do, do you?"

"Yes, I do." Bryn swiveled around to straddle Gunnar's thighs. He pulled Gunnar's hair loose from its messy bun. "I've been wanting to do this for so long." He ran his fingers through the long strands. "I knew it would be soft."

"You've been thinking about my hair?"

"Mmm."

Gunnar laughed. "You're full of surprises."

"And you're wasting time," Bryn countered. "What are you waiting for?"

Gunnar's gaze flicked to Bryn's lips, then back to his strange but beautiful eyes. He gripped Bryn's hips, steadying him. "I should still be mad with you."

"You can yell at me again later."

Gunnar leaned in and Bryn's teasing smirk gave way to a hopeful smile. "Stop talking." Gunnar brushed Bryn's lips with his own then deepened the kiss. Bryn melted into him and the kiss grew hungrier, more urgent. Gunnar didn't want it to end but it had to. He pulled away, breathless. Bryn's expression was one of dazed satisfaction.

"Better?" Gunnar asked.

Bryn laughed, his cheeks flushed. "Much better."

Before Bryn could say anything more, Gunnar pulled him back in, eager to taste him again. For a long time, they kissed and touched. There was nothing but sensation and desire until Bryn leaned his head on Gunnar's shoulder.

"I wondered if we'd ever get here," Bryn admitted, his voice quiet. "Not like this. This is everything."

"Sometimes, the best things come out of chaos."

"You're a poet now?"

"Just a wolf trying to make sense of it all," Gunnar replied. "I wasn't sure if I could do this — be this person. With you. For you."

"You've been this person since the day we met," Bryn said, "you just needed to let it happen." He entwined his fingers with Gunnar's. "And now you have. This is only the beginning."

"You seeing that in my head?"

"That and a whole lot more."

"You're blushing."

"Are you surprised? Your future intent is...stimulating." Bryn hid his face against Gunnar's chest. Gunnar wrapped his arms around him, holding him, feeling him breathe.

"We'll take it slow."

"Not too slow, though," Bryn whispered. "Kiss me again?"

"If you insist." That was a request Gunnar was more than happy to grant.

Sign up for our newsletter and find out about all our romance book releases, eBook sales and promotions, sneak peeks and FREE romance books!

Want to see more from this author? Here's a taster for you to enjoy!

The Augur: Seeing Blood
L.M. Somerton

Excerpt

"Why is it that Sunday afternoons always come around way too fast?" Bryn Ashton sat crossed legged on the floor of his bedroom, leaning back against the bed. "It's not fair." He shoved the last chunk of his candy bar into his mouth.

"Are you talking to yourself or me?" Gunnar Ericson, Bryn's lupine partner in the Gene Control and Research investigation team, loomed in the doorway.

Bryn balled up his candy wrapper then tossed it at the trash can. He missed. Gunnar snorted his amusement. Bryn glared at him. "Hey! Gimme a break. It's not easy aiming from down here, and I guess I was making a general statement of discontent."

"You couldn't hit a full-sized dumpster from three feet away and how many times in the last four months have we had a Sunday off?"

"Twice."

"Exactly, so be grateful that Warden was feeling generous and gave us today."

Bryn didn't want to think about their enigmatic, workaholic boss. "We could be doing something a lot more interesting. In your bed. Naked." Bryn eyed his partner's broad shoulders and long hair. His cock stirred. "I think we've mastered the art of kissing. Isn't it time we got to second base?"

"All in good time. As I keep telling you, a bit of anticipation doesn't hurt."

"That's a matter of opinion. You know I touch you all the time, right?" Bryn's augur abilities worked through touch and, from the start, Gunnar had never avoided it.

"Sure."

"So I know what your future intent is."

"Yeah."

"Gunnar!"

Gunnar chuckled. "Okay. Full disclosure. I'm not trying to tease you."

Bryn huffed. "Sure you're not."

"I don't want our first time to be here at headquarters. I can't wait to get my hands on you, but not here, where we work. It needs to be special."

"Oh my…you're a closet romantic!" Bryn scrambled to his feet.

"What's wrong with that?"

"Nothing." Bryn closed the gap between him and Gunnar. "It's sweet." He walked into Gunnar's arms.

"I am *not* sweet!"

Bryn tilted his head. "It's not a bad thing, even for a big bad wolf." He parted his lips. Gunnar took the hint and they were engaged in a satisfying kiss when his cell sounded. The ringtone was the theme from *Jaws*. Bryn rested his forehead against Gunnar's chest. "You have got to be kidding me. Warden."

"That man never takes a day off," Gunnar muttered, fishing his cell out of his pocket. "Ericson." He listened for a few seconds then the call ended. "In a shocking new development, we're wanted in the conference room."

"Well fuck. You gonna give me any more of a clue?" Bryn asked.

"He said, and I quote, 'get your asses downstairs now'. I don't know any more than you do."

Bryn sighed. "Let me grab my boots."

Five minutes later he was stomping down the stairs after Gunnar. He hadn't bothered with gloves or dark glasses because everyone in the building was used to his glowing eyes and knew better than to touch him. When they got to the conference room, Warden was waiting. Their admin assistant, Emmett Salisbury, hustled toward them from the direction of the staff entrance at the back of the building.

"Hey guys, what's up?" He shrugged off his yellow raincoat to reveal a red sweater vest and white shirt paired with blue jeans.

Bryn shrugged. "No idea but I think we're about to find out. No bow tie?"

"I was in a rush. I had plans to go out for tacos with Talbot." Talbot Dunne was Emmett's roommate and worked on the GCR's tech team.

"Bummer. Gunnar and I had plans too." Bryn grinned. Talbot blushed.

Bryn didn't know if their boss had another name to add to Warden, but he'd never dared ask. Warden sat at the head of the table dressed in an immaculate black suit, white shirt and subdued gray tie. He glanced at Bryn and frowned.

"Mr. Ashton, why do you always dress like an attendee at a goth rock concert?"

Bryn glanced down at his ripped black jeans and My Chemical Romance T-shirt. "Not sure I'd call this band goth rockers, sir…more like…uh, never mind." He sat his ass down before he got himself in more trouble. Warden's piercing stare was enough to curb even his tongue.

"Thank you for coming in, Emmett," Warden said in a much softer tone, bestowing Emmett with the trace of a smile. Emmett blushed even more then ducked his head. He pulled a notepad and pen from his satchel.

"No problem at all, sir."

"What's going on, boss?" Gunnar took the seat next to Bryn.

"Yeah, tell us, Warden. I had a fun evening in planned for my God-given, long-overdue day off." Bryn cast a sly look in Gunnar's direction.

"You need to readjust your priorities, young man. There are training courses for that," Warden replied.

"Why does that sound like a threat?"

"Because it is. Now shut up and listen." Warden's laser glare could have drilled a hole in sheet metal. "You'll all be aware that some gene-affected individuals spend time at The Facility undergoing a range of tests and personal development, mostly if they have chosen a career path in law enforcement or the military.

Bryn pressed his lips together in a tight line to stop yet another sarcastic remark. His own stay at The Facility had been lengthy, unpleasant and not exactly voluntary. *Would be so justified.*

"In the last six months I've been receiving disturbing reports that some of these individuals have been experiencing varied levels of psychosis. In the first instance, our scientists were concerned that this might be an effect of a new gene mutation but tests showed that was not the case. Blood samples, however, did reveal the presence of a narcotic. A new synthetic drug that we haven't come across before."

"Sounds nasty," Gunnar commented.

"Indeed. None of the people concerned were habitual drug takers so we weren't, and still aren't, sure how this got into their systems but the effects can be catastrophic. Enhanced abilities specific to both lupines and sanguines were found and, to start with, it appears that this is the only development but, after time, other traits begin to manifest."

Gunnar frowned. "Such as?"

"Paranoia, blood lust, increasing aggression and eventually hemorrhaging in the brain leading to death."

Emmett glanced up from his note taking, white-faced. "Who would do that to people?"

"Someone with no morals and zero compunction about using people for his own ends." Warden stood and clasped his hands behind his back. "Someone like Salvatore Russo."

"Wonderful," Bryn muttered. "The Hammer. Our favorite mob boss. Had to be him, didn't it. Only worse option would have been our neighborhood psycho pen pal, Dr. Templeton."

"Thank you for that observation, Bryn."

"How do you know it's him?" Gunnar asked.

"A better contribution, Detective. We know because last night, Boston PD raided what they thought was a meth lab. What they found was a production facility for this synthetic drug that the people they rounded up were calling Thanacrine. Several of those arrested have confirmed links with Russo."

"In Greek mythology, Thanatos was the personification of death," Emmett contributed. "He was a minor figure, often referred to but rarely appearing in person. That could be the root of the name."

"I thought Thanos was a Marvel character," Bryn said.

"Thanos was a warlord from Titan, whose objective was to bring stability to the universe by wiping out half of all life at every level no matter what it took…so he's a possible inspiration too," Emmett conceded.

"Thank you, Emmett," Warden said.

"So production has been stopped?" Gunnar asked.

"No. This was one small place. Russo isn't stupid. It's better to spread the risk across multiple facilities than concentrate efforts in a single location. Less of a financial hit if one place gets raided. There will be more."

"And he'll have another one up and running to replace this one before we can blink," Gunnar said. "So what's our interest?"

"Boston PD is handing the investigation over to us. We are better placed to make the connections between the people who've been affected and it falls within our remit. They'll continue to support when manpower is needed."

"That's a big case to take on."

"Which is why I've drafted in an additional resource to assist. Someone with first-hand knowledge of what's been happening." Warden avoided meeting Bryn's curious gaze.

Bryn leaned forward in his seat. "Tell me you fucking didn't…Warden…"

"Am I missing something?" Emmett asked.

"I really hope not," Bryn replied.

"This case demands the best we can offer." Warden stared at the door and without raising his voice said, "You can come in now." He rifled through a manila folder with the kind of forced casualness that set off every one of Bryn's finely tuned warning signals. Bryn braced for impact.

Giles Delacourt made his entrance. The sanguine moved with the kind of fluid grace that made catwalk models look clumsy. He was all long limbs and perfect posture in a charcoal suit that probably cost more than Bryn's monthly salary. His dark hair, shot through with elegant streaks of silver at the temples, was swept back from high cheekbones. He looked like he'd stepped out of a Renaissance painting, all aristocratic features and knowing eyes, with the kind of face that made people forget to breathe. The bright lighting should have made him look washed out. Instead, it seemed to create its own shadows around him, highlighting the sharp line of his jaw and the subtle curve of his mouth that always suggested he knew something Bryn didn't. Bryn's stomach knotted.

Warden actually stood up when Giles entered, like he was greeting nobility. Bryn remained exactly where he was. He'd learned the hard way that beauty could be the deadliest weapon in Giles Delacourt's arsenal. Gunnar was also on his feet, a warning growl rumbling in his throat. Bryn reached for his hand and tugged him back into his chair.

"Mr. Delacourt," Warden said, extending his hand. "Thank you for coming."

Giles took it with the kind of old-world courtesy that went out of style before the Industrial Revolution. "The pleasure is mine, Warden." His British accent was a smooth blend of old money and older privilege that made everything sound like poetry. Or a threat.

With Giles, it's usually both. Bryn's head throbbed. Separation hadn't dulled his memory of how that voice could make the most brutal lessons sound reasonable, even necessary. The way Giles could make breaking someone seem like an act of kindness.

Gunnar was bristling, his eyes dark with fury. Bryn was grateful, and though watching Gunnar rip Delacourt's head off would have been satisfying, violence wouldn't help the investigation. *I'm not even twenty-two, I shouldn't be expected to have achieved this level of restraint.*

Warden gestured for Giles to take a seat and resumed his own. Giles settled into one of the free chairs. His eyes, a shade of brown so dark they almost looked black, found Bryn's across the table. "Hello, dear boy. You're looking well."

Bryn had forgotten how much weight Giles could put into simple words, how he could make a casual greeting feel like fingers trailing down his spine. He didn't respond and gritted his teeth.

"Mr. Delacourt has been kind enough to offer his expertise on the Thanacrine case," Warden said.

"How generous of him," Bryn muttered.

Giles's lips curved. "Now, Bryn, there's no need for hostility. We're all on the same side here."

"Are we?" The words came out sharper than Bryn intended. The air in the room had that peculiar heaviness it always got around Giles, like the atmospheric pressure before a thunderstorm.

"Bryn," Warden said, his tone carrying a clear warning. "Mr. Delacourt has provided valuable intelligence about the effects of Thanacrine and has been conducting some investigations already. His knowledge could be crucial to locating more production facilities. He has agreed to assist us in a consulting capacity. He'll be working directly with you and Detective Ericson."

"That's not going to..." Bryn started, but Warden cut him off.

"This isn't a request. Whatever personal history exists between you and Mr. Delacourt is irrelevant to the current situation."

And you know all about that history. Bryn felt Giles' satisfaction like a physical thing, a cool current in the air. He gripped the arms of his chair until his fingers ached. He couldn't look at Gunnar.

"The latest batch is even more potent," Giles said. "The effects are devastating."

Don't fucking guilt trip me, you bastard.

Warden cleared his throat. "Allow me to introduce Detective Gunnar Ericson, Giles," he announced, gesturing at Gunnar, who offered a curt nod, his expression conveying his displeasure. "Gunnar is Bryn's partner."

"Protective. Interesting."

"And this is Emmett, our talented admin support."

Emmett glanced up from his laptop, his eyes wide behind his glasses. He blinked, and gave a shy, almost apologetic smile. "Uh, hi."

"Well then." Giles gave a lazy smile. "I'd say we're going to make quite the team. The dynamics will be *very* interesting."

The conference room felt smaller with each passing second. Bryn forced himself to take steady breaths, fighting the urge to bolt from his chair. He could feel Gunnar's concerned gaze, but couldn't bring himself to meet it. Not with Giles sitting there, radiating that infuriating calm. Bryn didn't want to give away how close he and Gunnar really were.

"Perhaps we should begin with what we know about the distribution network," Warden suggested, though his tone implied more of an order than a suggestion.

"I've managed to trace the probable routes of several shipments moving through the northeast corridor," Giles said.

"And you didn't think to share this information sooner?" Bryn couldn't keep the edge from his voice.

Giles' smile didn't waver. "Information gathering takes time, dear boy, even with the resources of The Facility to hand. Especially when one wishes to avoid detection. Mr. Russo's organization is…shall we say, particularly paranoid about new faces these days."

"I wonder why," Bryn muttered.

"Something to do with a recent court case, I understand," Delacourt said. "You'll have to tell me all about it."

Gunnar cut in before Bryn could say anything else. "Let's stick with this case, shall we? What's the delivery method?" he asked, his tone professional but cool. "If they're targeting gene-affected individuals specifically, they must have a way to ensure the drug reaches the right people."

"Ah, that's where it gets interesting." Giles pulled a small leather notebook from his jacket pocket. "They're using legitimate medical supply chains. Several private clinics that cater to our kind have been compromised. The drug is being administered through routine blood work and standard treatments. As you know, all sanguines and lupines are tested once a year as part of an ongoing national study. A trace of Thanacrine on the needle of a blood draw syringe is enough."

Emmett scribbled on his pad. "I can cross-reference clinic locations with reported cases when I have my laptop," he offered, not so shy with a challenge to work on.

"Good thinking." Warden nodded. "We need to identify any patterns in the targeting."

"There's more," Giles continued. "The clinics aren't random. They're all connected to a healthcare management company called Helix Solutions. On paper, it's a legitimate business. But dig deeper…" He slid a USB drive across the table to Emmett.

Bryn watched the drive move across the polished surface, his mind racing. "Helix Solutions. Why does that sound familiar?"

"Because" — Giles' eyes gleamed with something that might have been approval — "they received a rather substantial investment from one of Russo's shell companies six months ago. Something that was mentioned in the trial of Russo's accountant."

"Right before the first cases started showing up," Gunnar added, frowning.

"Indeed." Giles leaned back in his chair. "The question is, how deep does the infiltration go? How many medical professionals are knowingly involved, and how many are being used?"

"We need to get someone on the inside," Warden said, but Gunnar was already shaking his head.

"No way. It's too risky."

"Not necessarily." Giles' voice had that silken quality that always preceded his worst suggestions. "They're looking for gene-affected subjects. The drug doesn't touch anyone that isn't. We could send someone in for routine testing, or get someone employed at a clinic who's completely normal." He eyed Emmett.

"We need to think about the specifics," Warden said, breaking the tension. "Emmett, head up to your office and start running those clinic locations. Gunnar, I want you to pull everything we have on Helix Solutions. Talk to your contacts at Boston PD. And Bryn…" He paused, meeting Bryn's eyes with unexpected empathy. "I need you to work with Mr. Delacourt on identifying potential entry points. If anyone goes in, it'll need to be you because you'll have to read the staff somehow."

Bryn wanted to argue, but the weight of what they were dealing with settled over him. People were dying. His personal history with Giles didn't change that fact.

"Fine," he said, pushing back from the table. *Nothing about this is fine.* "But Gunnar takes the lead on planning."

"Of course," Giles agreed. "Shall we relocate or continue working here?"

"The conference room is needed," Warden said.

Gunnar shoved his chair back. "Our office is too small for all of us, but Emmett will need his equipment. We can use the table in our apartment. More space for mapping everything out."

"Very well," Giles acknowledged. "Lead the way, Detective Ericson."

As they filed out of the conference room, Bryn couldn't shake the feeling that they were walking into something potentially fatal. *Why does my life have to be so fucking complicated?* "This was supposed to be my day off," he muttered, not expecting sympathy from anyone.

About the Author

LM lives in a small village in the English countryside, surrounded by rolling hills, cows and sheep. She started writing to fill time between jobs and is now firmly and unashamedly addicted.

She loves the English weather, especially the rain, and adores a thunderstorm. She loves good food, warm company and a crackling fire. She's fascinated by the psychology of relationships, especially between men, and her stories contain some subtle leanings towards BDSM.

LM is a past winner of the National Leather Association – International's Pauline Reage Award for best novel and John Preston award for short fiction. She has twice won the Golden Flogger Award for best BDSM novel in the LGBT category. She has received multiple Honorable Mentions in the Rainbow Awards and won the Action and Adventure category of Divine Magazine's Book Awards.

L.M. Somerton loves to hear from readers. You can find her contact information, website details and author profile page at https://www.firstforromance.com

ENTWINED PUBLISHING

www.ingramcontent.com/pod-product-compliance
Lightning Source LLC
Chambersburg PA
CBHW020826260626
47169CB00003B/854